PRAISE FOR KATIE MAXWELL!

"Katie Maxwell has her finger on the pulse of teen girls and is well-versed in what's hot and what's not."

—*Roundtable Reviews*

WHAT'S FRENCH FOR "EW!"?

"Katie Maxwell deftly and hilariously delivers a potent message about the most important decisions. Emily is a breath of fresh air, wholly realistic, and utterly charming. If you love the Princess Diaries, this series is equally fun, no matter if you are a teen or once were one."

—*Huntress Reviews*

"The funniest book yet…"

—*RT BOOKclub*

THEY WEAR WHAT UNDER THEIR KILTS?

"Welcome back to the sidesplitting universe of Emily Williams…. [This is] a larky addition that won't disappoint teens hooked by the first book."

—*Booklist*

"A complete blast to read."

—*RT BOOKclub*

"A must-have book, as Emily's antics cannot be missed."
—Erika Sorocco, teen correspondent for *The Press Enterprise*

"Maxwell delivers a character that speaks her mind while making you laugh out loud…. Maxwell's novel is a real trip."

—*The Barnes & Noble Review*

BROWSERS' BOOKSTORE
121 NW 4TH STREET
CORVALLIS, OR 97330
WWW.BROWSERSBOOKSTORE.COM

MORE PRAISE FOR KATIE MAXWELL!

THE YEAR MY LIFE WENT DOWN THE LOO
"*The Year My Life Went Down the Loo* is a treat! Laugh-out-loud funny, full of sly wit and humor, poignant, realistic teenage angst, and expertly drawn characters, the book is impossible to put down."

—*Romance Reviews Today*

"Gripping, smart-alecky, shocking…and at the same time tender. A brilliant debut by Katie Maxwell!"

—*KLIATT*

"Refreshing. It's so true to life, dealing with an average teenage girl's issues instead of the mild and bland subjects covered in many other YA novels. Girls will laugh, sigh and squeal aloud as they embark upon Emily's journey."

—*RT BOOKclub*

"Girls of all ages will find themselves laughing out loud at Emily's crazy antics and experiences, but will also find themselves relating [to her]. A great start to a great new series."

—Erika Sorocco, teen correspondent for *The Press Enterprise*

THIS SUCKS!

I hesitated for a few seconds rather than running off, watched him roll on the ground clutching his groin, clearly in pain but not saying a single, solitary word. He was absolutely silent. The only other guy I've ever kneed (my first and only date) was screaming obscenities at me after I kicked him, but not Benedikt. Guilt washed over me as I watched, guilt and a horrible urge to laugh. Not at Benedikt, but at me, at my life. All I've ever wanted is to fit in, to be like everyone else, to not be the odd one, the one who is different from all the other kids, and what happens? I meet a vampire who tells me I'm the only one who can redeem his soul. Oh, yeah, like I bet *that* happens to every other girl who goes to Europe.

Other SMOOCH books by Katie Maxwell:
EYELINER OF THE GODS

The Emily Series:
THE TAMING OF THE DRU
WHAT'S FRENCH FOR "EW!"?
THEY WEAR *WHAT* UNDER THEIR KILTS?
THE YEAR MY LIFE WENT DOWN THE LOO

Got Fangs?

Katie Maxwell

SMOOCH **NEW YORK CITY**

To Michelle Grajkowski, the best agent a girl could have, and Vance Briceland, critique partner extraordinaire, both of whom managed to stay sane even when I was going nuts writing. Thanks, guys!

SMOOCH ®

January 2005

Published by

Dorchester Publishing Co., Inc.
200 Madison Avenue
New York, NY 10016

If you purchased this book without a cover you should be aware that this book is stolen property. It was reported as "unsold and destroyed" to the publisher and neither the author nor the publisher has received any payment for this "stripped book."

Copyright © 2005 by Marthe Arends

All rights reserved. No part of this book may be reproduced or transmitted in any form or by any electronic or mechanical means, including photocopying, recording or by any information storage and retrieval system, without the written permission of the publisher, except where permitted by law.

ISBN 0-8439-5399-3

The name "SMOOCH" and its logo are trademarks of Dorchester Publishing Co., Inc.

Printed in the United States of America.

www.smoochya.com

Visit us on the web at www.dorchesterpub.com.

Got fangs?

Chapter One

"What do you want to do first—have your aura photographed, or see the witch and have her cast a spell?" a girl asked.

You know that creepy kid who saw dead people in *Sixth Sense?* He's Norman P. Normal compared to me.

A guy wearing a backpack answered the girl's question. "I want to see the demonologist. I've had a bad run of luck lately; it could be due to demons. He can tell me if I've been demonized."

Okay, so the kid could see ghosts, I'll give him that, but was his mom a bona fide witch?

"I don't know that demons would give you bad luck, John," the girl said, frowning. "That sounds more like a curse. Maybe we should see the witch first and have her check you over for curses."

Did he spend his days traveling around Europe with a group of people who knew more about ghosts, demons, and various assorted weird things than stuff like ATM machines and cell phones and the latest hottie on *American Idol?*

1

The girl's voice cut through my mental rant. "I heard they have a vampire who drinks the blood of a volunteer each night! I'd love to see that!"

Oh, yeah, I forgot the vampires. Not that GothFaire had any, but still, what was I thinking?

"Hey, Lynsay, take a look at that girl. She looks odd. You think she's part of the show?"

I bet the *Sixth Sense* kid got to live in a normal home with a normal mom, and go to a normal school with other normal kids. Shoot, I'd be willing to put up with a little "I see dead people"-ing in order to have all that normal around me.

"Shhh, she might hear you."

The two people stopped in front of me, a girl and a guy probably a few years older than me using the opportunity to give me the once over. I tried to look like there wasn't anything unusual at all about standing in front of a tent with a big red hand painted on the side, shoving my own hands in my pockets just to make sure I didn't touch anything. Don't touch, don't tell; that's my policy.

"It's okay, she probably doesn't even speak English. She sure doesn't look normal, not with all that white skin and black hair. Maybe she's one of the Goths?"

Or maybe I just happen to have an Italian father and a fair-skinned Scandinavian mother? Ya think?

The girl giggled. I sent up a little prayer to the Goddess that Imogen would get her butt in gear and come back to her booth so I didn't have to stand here and let the rubes gawk at me.

Rube—that's one of those words you pick up when

you travel with a freak show. It means the uncool, people not hip to the way of the Faire.

"Maybe she's one of the vampires! She looks like one, don't you think? I can see her drinking your blood."

I turned my back so they wouldn't see me roll my eyes. It might be rare to find Americans this far into Hungary, but I wasn't so desperate to see my countrymen that I wanted to drink their blood. Besides, everyone knew only guys were vamps.

"Francesca, I'm so sorry!" Imogen hurried past the couple, her long blond hair streaming behind her as she dodged behind the table and grabbed the sign and easel that announced she was available to read palms and rune stones. She ignored the couple watching as she set the easel at the edge of the tent, popping the sign onto it as she chattered in her trademark Imogen style—breathy soft accent that was part British, part something I couldn't put my finger on, not that I'd been in Europe long enough to learn how to say anything more than: *hello, good-bye, thank you, how much is that,* and *I wouldn't let my dog use that toilet; where is a clean one?* in three different languages (German, French, and Hungarian, for those of you who are aching to know).

"Thank you so much for watching my things. Absinthe insisted on seeing me—evidently there's been another robbery. Oh, bless you, you didn't touch anything. You know I don't like anyone to touch the stones, and Elvis was after me again to help set up, which is ridiculous, because you know he has an orange aura, and orange auraed people are absolutely death to me before I'm supposed to read. But I have something exciting to tell you! My brother is coming to see me!"

I straightened up out of my perpetual slouch and gave the couple a big, toothy grin to show them I didn't have fangs. I was as tall as the guy (six feet), and as big as or bigger than him. He looked a little worried about that fact. The girl blushed a little and grabbed her boyfriend's arm, dragging him off toward the large tent, the one where the band plays after the magic shows.

The irony of me trying to prove I was normal didn't escape me. I'm like that. I see irony a lot. You know what? It's a pain in the butt. "They thought I was a vamp," I told Imogen as she shook out her blue casting cloth.

She cocked one golden eyebrow. "You? You're a female."

I resumed the slouch that made me look less like a burly football player, and tugged at my T-shirt in an attempt to make myself look smaller, prettier, thinner . . . you know, like a girl. "Yeah. Guess they don't know the rules."

She muttered something that sounded like *peons,* and arranged three ceramic bowls of rune stones along one side of the casting cloth. "Absinthe says the band ran off in the night with the last week's take, but Peter said they didn't, that only he and Absinthe know the combination to the safe, and that it wasn't forced. She's gone to Germany to find a new band."

I chewed on the chapped skin on my lower lip. This

was the third theft in the last ten days. Although I hated to agree with Absinthe, if the band skipped out during the night, it did sound like they were guilty. "What are they going to do about tonight?"

"Peter is hiring a local band. I hope they're good; the last few bands he's hired have been abysmal beyond belief."

I tipped my head to the side, tucking my hair behind my ear, wishing for the one thousandth time that it was anything but straight, straight, straight. Other people have curly hair—even my own mother has curly hair. Why can't I? "You're the only person I know who's heard Mozart play in person, and still thinks Goth bands are the best."

Imogen gave me one of her sly smiles. "Mozart was a brat. Gifted, but still a brat. But the Cure—now *that's* music!"

See what I'm talking about? Is it normal for your best girlfriend to be a four-hundred-year-old immortal?

"What's wrong, Fran? You look upset about something all of a sudden. Has Elvis been bothering you again? Would you like me to—"

I shook my head. "You know he doesn't see anyone but you. And besides, I'm bigger than him. I think he's afraid I'll beat him up if he tries to get busy with me."

Imogen stepped back from lighting scented candles, tipping her head as she looked me over. Her head tip was much nicer than mine, since she had long, curly hair, whereas I had a short, jaw-length pageboy full of straight black hair that refused either hot rollers or a perm's chemical wooing to give it body. "I see. You're feeling inadequate again."

I couldn't help but laugh at that. Nicely, because I like Imogen, but still, I had to laugh. "Again. Yeah, like when am I ever *not* inadequate?"

"I think the question is, rather, why do you feel you are?"

I glanced around to make sure no one was near to overhear us—not that some of the people connected with the GothFaire had to be near you to listen in (I'll bet you my whole summer's allowance that the *Sixth Sense* kid didn't have mind readers eavesdropping on *his* thoughts). "You want the list? You got it! First, I'm approximately the size and shape of your average high school linebacker."

"Don't be silly; you are not. You're a lovely girl, tall and statuesque. Men are going to be falling at your feet in a few years."

"Yeah, falling over in fright," I said, then quickly moved on before she was forced to say other nice things about me. You only have to look at me to see I am a big, hulking monstrosity. I didn't need tiny little petite pity from tiny little petite Imogen. "Second, my dad remarried a girl only a couple of years older than me, and told me he needed six months alone with her to get settled, which meant that when my mom took a job with a European traveling fair, I had to go with her."

"I'm sorry about your father," she said, her forehead all frowny, like it really mattered to her. That's one of the things I like so much about Imogen—she's honest. If she likes you, she *really* likes you, all of you, and stands up for you against who- or whatever is making your life a living nightmare. "That is wrong of him to banish you from his life. He should know better."

I made a face that my mother called a moue. "Mom says he's having a midlife crisis, and that's why he bought a sports car and got himself a trophy wife. It's okay. I didn't really like staying with him very much." *Bzzzt!* Big fat lie. I hoped Imogen's lie detector wouldn't catch me on that one. I hurried into the next complaint in case it did. "Third, the fair isn't a normal fair, the kind with popcorn and cotton candy and hokey country singers. Oh, no, this fair is filled with people who can talk to the dead, do real magic, read minds, and other weirdo stuff like that. One minute I had a relatively normal life with normal friends and a normal school, living with an almost normal mom in Oregon, and the next I'm Fran the Freak Queen, spending the summer hanging out with people who would give most people a case of the willies that would last them a lifetime. If *that* isn't something to look upset about, I don't know what is."

"The people here aren't freaks, Fran. You've been with us long enough to see that. They're gifted with rare talents, just as you are."

I stuffed my hands deeper into my pockets, the soft silk of the latex gloves brushing against my fingertips. My "talent" was something I didn't like talking about. To anyone, not that anyone but Imogen and my mom knew about it. I think Absinthe suspected, but she couldn't do anything about it. She was afraid of what Mom might do to her if she tried to mess with me.

Okay, sometimes it was handy having a witch for a mom. Most of the time it just sucked, though. What I wouldn't give for a mom who was a secretary and knew how to bake cookies. . . .

"You don't think *I'm* a freak, do you?" Imogen's blue eyes went black. That was one of the things her kind could do, she told me. Their eyes changed colors with strong emotions.

"No, not you, you can't help it if your dad was a vampire."

"Dark One," she corrected, fussing with the candles. They were special ones Mom made, invocation candles, bound with spells and herbs to enhance clarity of mind and communication with the Goddess.

I nodded. One of the first things Imogen had told me about the vamps was that they like to be referred to by their proper name: Moravian Dark Ones. Only the guys were Dark Ones, though; the women were just called Moravians. "You're not a freak just because your dad was damned by some demon lord. It's not like you drink blood or anything."

Imogen shrugged. "I have. It's not very good. I prefer Frankovka." That was Imogen's favorite wine, the only thing she drank. She had cases of the stuff she hauled around with her from town to town. She said it reminded her of her home in the Czech Republic. "I think, dear Francesca, that what you need most is a friend."

I kicked at a lump in the grass, and watched out of the corner of my eye as she made a few symbols in the air. Wards, she called them, protective devices like a spell that you had to draw in the air. All vamps—excuse me, *Moravians*—could draw wards. Mom had been nagging Imogen to teach her how to do it, but for some reason she had refused. "I've got friends, lots of friends."

That was another lie, I had no real friends back

home, but I figured I didn't need to make myself sound any more pathetic than I already did.

"Not in Oregon, here. You need friends here." She didn't look up as she traced another symbol into the casting cloth.

"I have friends here, too. There's you."

She smiled and beckoned me toward her. I leaned forward, the back of my neck tingling as her fingers danced in the air a few molecules away from my forehead. She'd drawn a protection ward for me once before, when I first arrived and Elvis—the resident flirtmeister—tried to hit on me. Having a ward protect you was a strange feeling, as if the air surrounding you were thick and heavy, like a cocoon. I'd never seen a ward actually work (Mom had a few words with Elvis, words like "manhood shriveling up and dropping off if you ever lay a finger on her"), but still, it was a nice gesture for Imogen to use up a little of her power on me. "I am flattered, Fran. You are, indeed, one of my best buds."

I tried not to smile. Imogen spoke like something out of an old English movie—very rich vowels, all proper and perfect grammar, with a lot of big words like a professor who dated Mom used, but mixed into that was a handful of hip slang that sounded odd in comparison. She didn't know that, though, and I didn't want to hurt her feelings. "And I like Peter, too. He's nice, when he's not groveling around Absinthe."

"Yes, he is. They are the strangest pair. . . ." She set the little box where she kept her reading money beneath the table, and dusted off the chair. "Did you know that they are twins?"

I shook my head. They didn't look like twins. Absinthe had pink hair, pencil-thin eyebrows, and a brittle smile, while Peter was short, balding, and had nice, gentle eyes. I had heard they had bought the Faire off of the group of people who used to work here, a group that scattered when it turned out the previous owners were psycho killers who had murdered a bunch of women all over Europe.

Do you wonder that I want to go home?

"They are, despite not looking like each other. It's almost as if one has all the good traits, and the other the regrettable ones."

I grinned after a quick check to make sure no one was nearby (you can't be too careful where Absinthe is concerned). "And then there's Soren. He's a friend, too."

"Yes, there is Soren," she said as she sat down, straightening her Stevie Nicks retro-seventies frilly lace shirt. I could tell she was trying not to look all-knowing, the way adults do whenever you talk about a guy your own age. The thing is, Imogen looks like she is just a few years older than me, about twenty, so sometimes I forgot that she'd lived as long as she has, making her more adult than any adult I knew. "He is a very sweet boy."

"He's okay," I said, really nonchalant. I didn't need Imogen telling everyone I had a crush on Soren. I didn't, in case you were wondering. Soren was fifteen (a year younger than me), had sandy hair and a face full of freckles, and was three inches shorter and probably fifty pounds lighter. He was, however, the only other person in the Faire who was close to my age, so we hung together.

"I think perhaps . . ." Imogen looked up and smiled brightly at three young women who approached her table. They asked her something in Hungarian, and after giving me an apologetic glance, she answered and waved them into the chairs on the opposite side of the table. Customers. I was a bit lonely and would have liked to stay and chat with Imogen, but one of the first things I'd learned when Mom dragged me here a month ago was that paying customers came first. I gave Imogen a little wave and went off to see what Soren was up to.

The GothFaire is usually set up in a basic U shape, with the big tent at the bottom of the U, and two long wings containing the individual tents, with all the "talent" along one side, and vendor tents along the other. The tents weren't camping tents; they were made of heavy canvas, painted in wild colors with even wilder designs, all of them open-fronted, some also having wooden panels for strength. Most could be quickly set up or torn down, and packed into long canvas bags. Soren mostly helped with the setting-up and tearing-down part, but he also did odd jobs, stuff his dad (Peter) was supposed to do, but never had time to get done.

I wandered down the line of tents, weaving in and out of the early Fairegoers, listening to, but not understanding, the different languages around me. The big lights lining the aisles had been turned on, since the sun had just gone down, casting eerie shadows in the little dips and hollows of the grassy field that held the Faire. Enticing, spicy scents came from the food-vendor tents, blending with the faint lingering smell of the sun-warmed earth beneath my sandals. I waved at Mom as she counseled someone with a spell. Davide, her cat, sat looking like a black meat loaf on her table, his front paws tucked under his chest, his white whiskers twitching as he watched me walk by. Davide doesn't really like me, but I put up with him mostly because I like cats, but also because Mom said he was very wise.

A cat. Wise. What*ever.*

I found Soren down with a bunch of guys in matching denim jackets unloading amps and sound equipment from a battered old truck. The replacement band had arrived.

"Hey," I said.

"Hey," Soren said back. We're cool that way.

"What's the band called?" I asked as he struggled with an amp that was almost as tall as he was. I hefted one side of it onto my shoulder and helped him ease it off the truck and onto a dolly.

"Crying Orcs. They look great, don't they?"

We both looked at the guys clustered around a soundboard. I shrugged. "They look like all the other bands." I'd die before I admitted it, but Goth wasn't really my style. I was a ballad girl. I liked Loreena McKennitt and Sarah McLachlan, women like them. Guys singing about wanting to slash someone's wrists and watch their blood drip away forever just left me kind of cold.

"I heard them last night. They're good. You'll like them." I shrugged again. "Take this in for me, please. Give it to Stefan; he's the man with one ear."

Soren dumped a heavy coil of cable in my arms. I grunted a little when he did. Darned thing weighed a ton. I carefully edged around the amps, stacks of sound equipment, and assorted crates, and stepped out into the alley between the truck and the tent.

Right into the path of a motorcycle.

Chapter Two

"Narng."

Darkness swirled through my head, but it wasn't the familiar darkness of the inside of my eyelids, or even the twice-experienced darkness of anesthesia, but a really black darkness that was filled with sorrow . . . and concern.

Are you injured? Does anything hurt?

"Gark," I said. At least I think it was me, I felt my lips move and all, but I don't think I've ever said the word "gark" before in my life, so really, why would I be saying it now, to this sad blackness that talked directly into my head?

Gark. I'm not familiar with that word. Is it something new?

"Mmrfm." Yep, that was me speaking, I recognized the "mmrfm." I said that every morning when the clock radio went off. I'm a heavy sleeper. I hate being woken up.

You don't look injured. Did you strike your head?

The motorcycle! I had been run over. I was probably dead. Or dying. Or delirious.

You stepped directly in front of me. I had no time to avoid you. You really should learn to look before you walk out from behind trucks.

You shouldn't have been driving so freakin' fast, I thought back to the voice that rubbed like the softest velvet against my brain, not in the least bit surprised or shocked or even weirded out that someone could talk to me without using words. I'd been with the GothFaire for a whole month. I've seen stranger things.

The voice smiled. I know that sounds stupid, because how can a voice smile, but it did. I felt the smile in my head just as clearly as I felt the hands running down my arms, obviously checking me over for injury.

Eeek! Someone was touching me! The second my hands were touched . . .

My brain was flooded with images, like a slide show of strange, unconnected moments in time. There was a man in one of those long, ornately embroidered coats like Revolutionary guys wore. This guy was waving his arms around and looking really smug about something, but just as soon as I got a good look at him, he dissolved into mud and rain, and blood dripping from a dead guy in World War I clothes. He was sprawled backward in a ditch, his eyes open, unseeing as the rain ran down from his cheeks into his hair. It was night, and the air was full of the smell of sulfur and urine and other stuff that I didn't want to identify. That dissolved, too (thank goodness), this time into a lady with a huge, and I mean *huge,* like a yard-high, powdered white wig and a giganto-hipped dress with her boobs almost popping out of it. She was lifting up the bottom of her skirt, peeling it back slowly, exposing her leg as if it were something special (it wasn't), saying something in French about pleasure.

I jerked my hand back from the man touching it at the same time I opened my eyes. Vampire. Moravian. Nosferatu. Dark One. Call him what you want; this man was a bloodsucker.

His eyes met mine and I sucked in my breath.

He was also the cutest guy I had ever seen in my whole entire life. We're talking open-your-mouth-and-let-the-drool-flow-out cute. We're talking hottie. Major hottie. The hottest of all hotties. He wasn't just good-looking; he was fall-to-the-ground-dead gorgeous. He had brown-black hair pulled back into a ponytail, black eyes with lashes so long it made him look like he was wearing mascara, a fashionable amount of manly stubble, and he was young, or at least he looked young, maybe nineteen. Twenty at the most. Earrings in both ears. Black leather jacket. Black tee. Silver chain with an ornate Celtic cross hanging on his chest. Oh, yes, this was one droolworthy guy bending over me, and just my luck, he was one of the undead.

"Some days I just can't win," I said, pushing myself into a sitting position.

"Some days I don't even try," he answered, his voice the same as the one that had brushed my mind. It was faintly foreign, not German, like Soren's and Peter's, but something else, maybe Slavic? I haven't been in Eastern Europe long enough to be able to tell accents very well, and since everyone in the Faire speaks English, I haven't really had to learn much. "You are unhurt."

"Was that a question or a comment?" I asked, ignoring his hand as I got to my feet, brushing off my jeans and testing my legs for any possible compound fractures or dismemberment or anything like that.

"Both." He stood up and flicked the dirt and grass off my back.

"Oh, lucky me, I got to be run over by a comedian," I growled. "Hey! Hands to yourself, buster!"

His hand, in the act of brushing grass off my legs, paused. Both of his eyebrows went up. "My apology."

I tugged down my T-shirt and gave him a look to let him know that he might be a vamp, but I was on to him. That was when it struck me that I had to look up to glare at him. Up. As in . . . up. "You're taller than me."

"I'm glad to see that you aren't suffering any brain damage. What is your name?"

"Fran. Uh . . . Francesca. My dad's parents are Italian. I was named for my grandma. She's in Italy." God, could I sound any more stupid? Babbling, I was positively babbling like an idiot, to a man who at some point in his life had a big-haired French Revolution babe baring her legs at him. *Oh, brilliant, Fran. Make him think you're a raving lunatic.*

"That's a very pretty name. I like it." He smiled when he said that last bit, showing very white teeth. Nonpointy teeth. As in no fangs. I wanted to ask him what happened to his fangs, but Soren and some of the band guys had just noticed us standing with the cable spilled all over, and the motorcycle lying on its side.

"Fran, are you all right?" Soren asked, jumping off the truck and limping toward me. One leg is shorter than the other, but he's really touchy about his limp, so we don't say anything about it.

The vamp glanced at Soren, then back at me. "Boyfriend?"

I snorted, then wished I hadn't. I mean, how uncool is snorting in front of a vamp? "Not! He's younger than me."

"Is something wrong, Fran?" Soren said, limping up really quickly, giving the dark-haired guy a look like he was trying to take a favorite toy away. To tell you the truth, I was kind of touched by the squinty-eyed, suspicious look Soren was giving the guy.

"It's okay, I was just run over. The cable isn't hurt, though."

"Run over?" Two of the band guys hurried around Soren and grabbed the cable, examining the ends of it.

"Joke, Soren. I'm not hurt. This is Imogen's brother."

The dark-haired vamp gave me a curious look before holding out his hand to Soren. He didn't deny it, so I gathered my guess was right. It was no surprise, though. I mean, how many authentic Dark Ones were going to be hanging around the Faire on the very same evening Imogen was expecting her brother? "Benedikt Czerny."

"Chairnee?" I asked.

"It's spelled C-Z-E-R-N-Y. It's Czech."

"Oh. That's right, Imogen said she's from the CR. How come her last name is Slovik?"

"Females in my family take their mother's surname," Benedikt said smoothly, then pulled his bike upright. He was talking about Moravians. I wondered if anyone else knew what he really was. Imogen said only Absinthe knew about her—I had discovered it by accident one night when we both reached for the same piece of berry cobbler and my hand brushed hers.

"I'm Soren Sauber. My father and aunt own the GothFaire."

Soren had puffed himself up, his normally nice blue eyes all hard as he glared at Benedikt. I'd never seen him like that; usually he was all smiley and friendly, kind of like a giant blond puppy who wants to tag along.

"It is a pleasure to meet you," Benedikt said politely. He turned to me and offered his hand.

I stuck mine behind my back. "Sorry, I have this thing about touching people. It's . . . uh . . . a skin problem." A skin problem. *A skin problem!* Great, now he'd think I had leprosy or something.

His left eyebrow bobbled for a moment before it settled down. He looked back at Soren. "Is there somewhere I can park . . . ? Yes, I see. Thank you." His black eyes flickered over to me. I sucked in my cheeks and tried to look like I wasn't the sort of leprosy-riddled babbling idiot who walks out in front of motorcycles. "I look forward to seeing you both again."

"Wow," I said as he walked his bike over to where a horse trailer was parked next to Peter and Soren's bus. "Is he, like, major cool, or what?"

"Major cool?" Soren looked after Benedikt. The guy had a really nice walk. I mean, *niiiiiiice*. Course, his skintight black jeans didn't hurt any. "I suppose so."

I hugged my arms around my ribs, vaguely surprised that they didn't hurt despite my being slammed to the ground. Nothing on me hurt. To tell the truth, I felt kind of . . . tingly.

"You should stay away from him," Soren said. I dug the latex gloves out of my pocket and put them on, then pulled the black lace gloves from my back pockets. I had bought them from one of the vendors because they looked suitably Goth. No one would look twice at someone wearing black lace gloves, but experience taught me that if you go around wearing latex doctor's gloves, people start to give you strange looks. Soren watched me put on the gloves without saying anything. I told him I had hypersensitive skin (not terribly far from the truth) the first day we met, and he's never said anything about my gloves since. I guess what with his limp, he figured it wasn't kosher to comment on my gloves.

"Why? He seemed okay to me."

"I don't like him. You should stay away from him. He could be . . . dangerous."

I grinned and socked him on the shoulder in a friendly buddy sort of way. "Yeah, right, I know the truth; you're jealous."

His eyes got all startled-looking. "What?"

"His bike. You're jealous 'cause he came roaring up on a big Harley or whatever it is, and your dad won't let you get a Vespa until you're sixteen."

He just stared at me for a second, then turned back to the truck. "Are you going to help unload or not?"

"Sure." I smiled to myself. Guys hate it when you get them pegged so quickly. I spent the next hour helping the band set up behind the big black curtain that hid the back of the stage from the front, where the magic acts were held. GothFaire got two basic kinds of customers—average people who were excited to see a traveling fair come to town (and we went to some really small towns)—people who wanted to have their palms read and fortunes told, and buy some crystals and aura pictures and all that cheesy stuff—and the rockers who traveled from around whatever country we were in to hear the bands. The last band we had was from Holland and they were really popular, bringing in lots of people for the shows, but as the Crying Orcs were local boys, I figured the crowd wouldn't be as big for them.

I wandered around for a bit, watching the visitors (they were much more interesting than the people they came to see), more than a little bored. I thought about going to see if Tallulah had manifested any interesting ectoplasm (lately it's all been coming out in the shape of Matt Damon—she's got a bit of a crush), when I realized that it was a quarter to eleven. I hung around the outside of my mother's tent until her customer went off clutching a bottle of happiness.

(Mom's most popular potion—it really works, too. I drank a big jug of it when I just learned how to crawl. She said I laughed for a week straight.)

"Franny, could you watch things for a couple of minutes? I have a few premade vials of happiness and luck, but ran out of blessings. I'll just run to the bathroom and be back in two shakes of a cat's tail."

I swear Davide rolled his eyes. "Sure, no problem. Hey, Mom, do you know anything about Imogen's brother?"

"Imogen's brother? I didn't know she had a brother. Now, where did I put those keys . . . ?" She bent over, searching through the huge mom-bag she carries, looking for the keys to our trailer. The first week we were here, when I was going through the horrible shock of having to move from our nice house outside of Portland to a small trailer in the middle of Germany, she told me I could pick out what to paint on the trailer. Everyone in the Faire had their trailer painted with their own emblems on it. Imogen's was gold and white, with scarlet hands and runes. Absinthe's was pink and green (a horrible combination), while Soren and Peter's bus-turned-into-home-on-wheels was a soft sky blue with a castle and knights on horseback stretching down the length. Soren told me the town in Germany where he was born had a big ruined castle that he used to love playing in.

Mom wanted a representation of the Goddess on ours. I decided on a midnight-blue background with gold stars and crescent moons on it. She put all sorts of metaphysical meaning into it, saying I had chosen to portray the mystery of the unknown, yadda yadda yadda.

I just thought it was pretty.

"Drat it all, I know I had my keys when I left the trailer; I remember locking up after you left. Honey?"

"I gave you my keys two days ago, Mom. Don't tell me you've lost those, too?"

"Bullfrogs!" Mom takes this witch stuff seriously. She doesn't swear, because most swear words have their origins in curses, and she won't dabble in anything dark like a curse. She practices only good magic. It gets a bit tedious sometimes. I mean, I could have really used a couple of quality curses during my sophomore year.

She held out her hand. "Would you?"

"Mom!"

"Please."

"I am not the Clapper! You'll have to find your own keys."

"I know, baby, but I have to use the bathroom, and I want to change into my invocation gown. Just this once, please?"

I turned my back to the opening of the tent so no one would see me as I peeled off the lace glove, then the latex one beneath it. "You know I hate doing this. It makes me feel like a big fat freak."

"You're not big or fat or a freak; you've been blessed by the Goddess."

I took a deep breath and tried to clear my mind, like she said I was supposed to do in order to open myself up to all the possibilities. "Is anyone looking?"

"Not a soul."

I took her hand in mine, and tried to ignore the rush of thoughts that filled my mind. Mom arguing with Absinthe about the band stealing the Faire money. Her worries about me not being happy here battling with her desire to be with the Faire, all mixed up with the fear that the Faire would close if the thefts didn't stop. Her pain over Dad remarrying so quickly after the divorce. The sudden thought that she hadn't changed Davide's litter box, a growl of hunger, a sense of loneliness that so closely resembled my own that I almost dropped her hand . . . I gritted my teeth and tried to focus my mind to pick through hers until I found what I wanted to know.

"You dropped them just outside of the trailer. They're in a tall clump of grass beneath a candy wrapper," I said, letting go of her hand with a sigh of relief. Mom was the only person I could touch who didn't leave me feeling all creepy . . . until Benedikt. I blinked at that thought, and realized it was true. Touching him didn't freak me out like it did when I touched anyone else—he was warm and soft, inviting, a bit mysterious, but oddly comfortable, considering I'd only just met him.

And, of course, there was the fact that he was a vampire.

"You're such an angel," Mom said, kissing my forehead and rushing off to the trailer, pausing to tell the group of people approaching the tent that she'd be back in ten minutes.

"If I'm an angel, where are my wings?" I whispered. It was what I always said whenever she called me an angel, starting from the time when I was little and she would swing me around and around, and tell me I was an angel sent to bring heaven to earth.

I looked down at my hand. It wasn't small and slender like hers, or long and graceful like Imogen's. It was big, and my fingers had blunt tips. A musician's hand, someone had once told me, but I had to stop piano lessons when I was twelve because I couldn't stand touching Mrs. Stone's piano. Too many kids used it for their weekly lessons—I'd go home afterward shaking and near tears. That was when Mom finally figured out what had happened to me.

"How long have you been a psychometrist?"

I turned around slowly, wondering if Benedikt had read my mind.

"Since I was twelve."

He stood on the other side of the table, a large black shape blocking my view of the sky turned indigo and black. "Puberty?"

I nodded and tried to look away, but couldn't. It was something about his eyes, glowing with an inner light as they watched me fiddle with my gloves. I didn't want to talk to him about the weird things I could do. I didn't want him to think I belonged in the freak show.

You're not a freak.

"Stop that," I said, taking a couple of steps backward, as if distance would keep him out of my mind.

Are you afraid of me?

His eyes were the color of dark oak, little golden flecks against the warm honey brown, flecks I could see even though his face was thrown into shadow.

"Why should I be afraid of you? If anyone should be afraid, it's you. I know your secret."

And I know yours, he said into my head as he started coming toward me.

I backed up a couple more steps, straightening my shoulders, trying to look big and tough and mean. "Yours is worse than mine, so if you don't want to end up on the business end of a sharp stake, you'd just better back off and leave me alone."

I don't want to leave you alone.

"You don't know who you're messing with—" I started to say, then shrieked when he lunged toward me, grabbing my arms and pulling me toward him. We stood together like that for a second, me braced and ready for him to bite me, him looking down on me with eyes that were changing into glittering ebony.

"I don't want to mess with you at all, Fran." Slowly, very slowly, his hand slid down my arm. I watched it as it headed for my naked hand, my bare hand, my hand that kept me from being happy like any other kid.

"Don't," I said, ashamed it came out a whimper.

"Trust me," he said softly. His fingers trailed along the back of my bare hand, then curved under, pushing my arm up so that our palms rested together. I gasped and held my breath, waiting for the rush of images, waiting for the *everything* that would pour from his mind into mine.

There was nothing. I was touching him, hand to hand, and I felt nothing, saw nothing.

I looked from our hands to his face. "How do you do that? How do you turn yourself off like that?"

His fingers twined through mine, and all of a sudden I was aware that he was a guy and I was a girl, and we were standing together holding hands.

"You know who I am."

"I know what you are, if that's what you mean."

He nodded. "What do you know about us?"

"I know that you're a vampire . . ." His fingers tightened on mine. *Poop. Used the V-word.* ". . . but that you prefer to be called Dark Ones. I know that you drink people's blood to survive, and you're probably a couple of hundred years old—is Imogen your older sister, or younger?"

"Older."

I don't know why that made me feel better, considering he was probably at least three hundred years old, but it did. "And I know that you are really sad most of the time, but somehow, you can block the images in your mind from me at the same time you can talk into my head."

"Do you know anything about how a Dark One is created? How he can be redeemed?"

"Um . . . you're created . . . something about a demon lord cursing you?"

I thought his eyes were black before, but they went absolutely obsidian. "My father was cursed by a demon lord."

"Oh, that's right, Imogen said something about the sins of the father being passed on to the sons, but not the daughters. I don't know anything about redemption."

He looked at our hands, still locked together. It was strange touching him, feeling his warm fingers twined through mine, and not having my head filled with his thoughts and memories and everything else I felt when I touched people. "For every Dark One there is one woman, called a Beloved, who can redeem his soul, a woman who can balance his darkness with her light, and make him whole again."

"Oh," I said. So it wasn't the smartest thing I could say. The guy was holding my hand—it was hard to think about anything but how warm his hand was.

"You are my Beloved."

I snatched my hand out of his, jumping backward straight into the metal rods that held the tent up. The pointy bit of bone on my wrist whacked into it, making me yelp in pain. "You're crazy!" I said as I rubbed my sore wrist. "You're psycho! You're a total nutball! You're some sort of stalker!"

He stepped forward. "I don't have a choice in the matter. Dark Ones have only one Beloved—many never find them. I had almost given up hope that I would ever find mine. Let me see your wrist."

"Why, so you can bite it? No! I don't want you touching me. You're some sort of weirdo vamp perv. Leave me alone."

"I swear to you I will not hurt you, and that I am not a weirdo vamp perv. Let me see your wrist."

He stood in front of me, close enough to grab my wrist but not touching me, just waiting for me to offer up my wrist like a good little sheep.

I am *so* not a sheep.

I made a fist with my right hand at the same time I stomped on his foot as hard as I could, kneed him in the happy sacs, and as he doubled over to clutch his crotch, punched him in the Adam's apple like Mom showed me in case some guy ever got nasty with me.

I just don't think she anticipated that guy being a vamp.

Chapter Three

I know what you're thinking. You're thinking, *Hey, I didn't know you could bring a vampire to his knees by kicking him in the noogies.*

Well, you can. I mean, they might be the walking undead and all that, but they are just guys, you know? They have the same outdoor plumbing as nonvamp guys, and I gathered from the way Benedikt writhed around on the ground that getting whomped there hurt him just as much as it would a normal guy.

Which is probably why I hesitated for a few seconds rather than running off, watching him roll on the ground clutching his groin, clearly in pain but not saying a single, solitary word. He was absolutely silent. The only other guy I've ever kneed (my first and only date) was screaming obscenities at me after I kicked him, but not Benedikt. Guilt washed over me as I watched him, guilt and a horrible urge to laugh. Not at Benedikt, but at me, at my life. All I've ever wanted is to fit in, to be like everyone else, to not be the odd one, the one who is different from all the other kids, and what happens? I meet a vamp who tells me I'm the only one who can redeem his soul. Oh, yeah, like I bet *that* happens to every other girl who goes to Europe.

"I just want a normal life," I yelled at Benedikt. "Is that so wrong? I am *not* Buffy the Vampire Slayer!"

A little grunt escaped him as he got to his knees. "Good. I'm not up to playing Angel if you're going to be attacking me very often."

I stood at the front of the tent, part of me twitching to get away from him, the other part wanting to apologize. All he had done was be nice to me, and I repaid that kindness by kicking him where it counts. *Oh, good one, Fran.*

"You watch *Buffy*?" my stupid mouth asked. It was like I was possessed or something. I should have been running or apologizing, not standing there talking TV with an honest-to-Goddess Moravian Dark One. "Which season was your fave?"

"Third." He got to his feet, breathing heavily as he stood doubled over, his hands on his knees.

"Oh. I like the fourth. Spike rocks." He didn't say anything, just slowly straightened up until he was standing more or less normally. "Um. Are you okay?"

He nodded, his hand twitching like he wanted to rub himself but couldn't because I was there. I felt guiltier than ever.

"I'm sorry."

I stared at him, blinking like an idiot. "What?"

"I said I'm sorry."

I blinked even more until I realized what I was doing. "You're apologizing to me? For what?"

"Frightening you. I shouldn't have dumped it all on you so soon."

"Oh." My inner Fran, the annoying one who always tries to make me do the right thing, nudged me hard. "Um. I'm sorry, too. I didn't mean to hurt you. Well, I did because you were getting bossy with me, but now I'm sorry you did. I mean, I'm sorry I did. We both did." Great, now I sounded like a lunatic. If he was in any doubt that I was the queen freak of all freaks before, he wouldn't be now. A lunatic freak.

"You're not a freak," he said tiredly, like it was something he said a lot.

"Will you stop that! No one gets into my mind unless I invite them."

"I'm sorry," he said again, and rubbed his neck.

Before I knew what I was doing, I stepped forward and touched the red mark on his neck where I had hit him. He stood still, his hands at his sides as I gently felt around his Adam's apple. His skin was warm. "I thought vamps were supposed to be dead. How come you're warm?"

He placed my hand on his chest, over his heart. I could feel it thumping away in there just like anyone else's heart. "Do I feel dead?"

"No." I let my fingers wander over to the silver Celtic cross that hung from his neck. "You can wear a cross."

"I can."

"You're not dead and you can wear a cross." I gave

him my best squinty eyes. "Are you sure you're a Dark One?"

Quite sure. He laughed into my mind.

"Hey!"

He held up a hand and grinned. "Sorry. Won't happen again. Not unless you invite me first."

"It'd better not." I took a step back and nibbled my lip as I looked at him. "How come you're not mad at me for hitting you?"

"I frightened you. I don't blame you for what you did."

"Why not?"

His eyes had lightened while we were talking, but they suddenly went black again. He didn't say anything.

"Anyone else would have been pissed at me, but you're not. Why? Because you think I'm you're salvation?"

He just stood there, one hand in his jeans pocket, the other hanging open and relaxed, his eyes glittering like those shiny black stones Mom sometimes uses— hematite, they're called.

"I'm sixteen, Ben."

His eyebrows raised. "Ben?"

"Benedikt is kind of a mouthful."

He smiled. "I know how old you are."

"I don't even want a boyfriend, let alone to get married to you or whatever it is you Moravians do to get your soul back. I just want to be left alone. I just want to get through this summer so I can go live with my dad in the fall and go to school and not have to travel all over Europe with Mom tutoring me, like she's threatening to do. Besides, you're . . . you're . . ." I stopped. I'd rather die than tell him that he was so gorgeous he probably had to pry the girls off him with a two-by-four, whereas I was . . . me. Okay, people didn't actually barf when they saw me, but I was *not* gorgeous.

"I'm what?"

I shrugged. "A vamp."

He tucked one side of my hair behind my ear. It was an oddly intimate gesture, and left me feeling hot, then cold, then hot again. "I don't want anything from you, Fran. The only reason I told you that you were my Beloved is so you understand that you can trust me. A Dark One can never harm his Beloved."

"Oh, really? So if I had a stake and started pounding it on your chest, what would you do?"

He pursed his lips as he thought it over. He looked so funny, I couldn't keep from smiling. "Depends. Where would you be pounding?"

"Right over your heart."

"Then I'd die."

My smile faded. "Really? The stake thing works?"

"Yes, it works. So does beheading."

"And you'd let me kill you? You'd just stand there and let me kill you?"

He nodded. "If it was in your heart to see me dead, yes, I'd stand there and let you kill me."

Wow. Talk about a head trip. I decided I wasn't ready to think about that and pushed it aside. "How about sunlight?"

He made a face. "It wouldn't kill me, not unless I

34

was out in it for several hours, but I do my best to avoid it. Gives me a hell of a sunburn."

"Huh." I looked him over. He'd taken his leather jacket off earlier and was now wearing a sleeveless black tee. His arms were tan. So was his face. He had a tattoo of words in a fancy script twined around in a circle on his shoulder. "So, what, they have Moravian sunlamps to keep you from looking fishbelly white?"

He laughed. I liked it; it was a nice laugh. It made me want to laugh, too.

"Something like that." He looked over my shoulder, then bent down to pick up the gloves I had dropped, handing them to me as he added, "Maybe we can talk about this another time."

"Sure. I promise I won't hit you again." I meant it, too. It might be stupid to believe what he said about not stopping me if I wanted to kill him (as if!), but I did believe him when he said he wouldn't hurt me.

He started toward me, toward the exit behind me. I chewed on my lip for a few seconds before I blurted out, "Would you take me for a ride on your bike?"

He was right next to me when he paused. His eyes were back to their normal dark oak color, the gold flecks clearly visible as he stared down at me; then they lifted to look beyond me. "If your mother says it's all right, yes."

I turned to see what he was looking at. Mom stood in the entrance to the tent, dressed in her white-and-silver invocation gown, the layers of light gauze fluttering around behind her in the breeze. She had a crown of white flowers in her hair, ribbons trailing down her back. In one hand, on a piece of scarlet velvet, she held her silver scrying bowl; in the other were a handful of invocation candles. Davide sat next to her, his mouth open in a silent hiss at Ben.

I sighed and plopped myself down in the nearest chair. Why did I even try to act normal when everyone around me was so weird?

Mom grilled me about Ben for the rest of the night and most of the next morning. Who was he, what did he want, why had I mentioned hitting him, yadda yadda yadda. I answered her questions because it was the first normal mom-type thing she'd done since I was in the sixth grade, and reassured her that she didn't need to cast a spell on Ben (not that I was sure it would work—maybe Dark Ones are spell-resistant? I'd have to ask Imogen).

Then she started in on stuff that really made me uncomfortable.

It was around eleven in the morning. We had just gotten up (the GothFaire closes at two in the morning during the summer), and Mom was standing at the tiny little stove that she sometimes cooked on. When she absolutely had to. She may be a great witch, but she's a pretty bad cook. Usually I do it, but this morning I had been too busy being grilled about Ben.

"I don't like the thought of you seeing a boy that much older than you," she said once she started to wind down.

"I'm not seeing him; we were just talking." Yeah,

okay, so he expected me to salvage his soul at some point, but hey, that didn't mean we were dating or anything, right? "Is there any more hot water?"

Mom shook the electric teakettle and handed it over to me. I made another cup of tea (Earl Grey—I may be a freak, but I'm a civilized freak) and squeezed a quarter of a lemon into it.

"How old is he?"

I looked at her over the top of my mug. She was standing in front of the stove alcove, poking at some fruit hanging from a wire basket. The trailer we shared had one bedroom (hers) and a second bed (where I slept) that was converted from the tiny table and couch I was sitting at now. Mom has a very good lie radar. I figured she was suspicious enough without my saying something that would get her undies in a bunch. "Um . . . he's younger than Imogen."

"Is he? Then he must be about eighteen or nineteen." *Give or take a couple of hundred years, yeah.* "That's still too old for you. I'll have a little chat with him. What would you say to French toast this morning?"

Now *my* radar went off. She was offering to make me breakfast? "Sounds good. You don't have to talk to Ben, Mom. I'm not dating him or anything."

"Mmm. Do we have any eggs?"

"In the fridge." I watched her for a few minutes as she hummed a little song to herself while she whipped up a couple of eggs, sniffed a small carton of milk and decided it wasn't too old, added a sprinkle of cinnamon, then started slicing thick slabs of bread from the loaf she'd picked up a half hour earlier. "Okay. What are you up to?"

She turned around to look at me, her eyebrows doing a pretty good job of looking surprised. "What do you mean?"

"You're cooking breakfast. You never cook breakfast for me."

"I most certainly do! I cooked breakfast for you just last . . . last . . ."

"Uh-huh. You can't remember, can you? It's been that long."

She waved an eggy spatula at me. "I remember like it was yesterday. It was when you broke your arm riding your bike to school. I made you eggs Benedict. You loved it."

I smiled into my tea. "Mom, I was in the fifth grade then."

She turned back to the stove with a self-righteous sniff. "I merely pointed out that I have, upon occasion, made you breakfast."

"Usually only when you want something from me, so dish. What do you want me to do? If it involves dressing up as a naiad and frolicking around a stream like you made me do last summer, the answer is no. One round of poison ivy is enough to last me a lifetime."

She flipped the French toast in the skillet, not saying anything until she put it on a plate and handed it to me. To my surprise, she sat down across the table rather than making a plate for herself. "Franny, I'm worried about the Faire. It's these thefts—if they continue, the Faire will go bankrupt, and we'll have to go home."

Home! Oh, man, how I wanted to go home! Home

to our little house with the tiny little flower garden,
home to my room with the two leaks when it rained
hard, home to everything familiar and normal, where I
had my place and no one bothered me in it. Home
sounded just fine to me.

Unfortunately, Mom didn't feel the same way. She'd
signed a year's contract to tour with the Faire, dis-
pensing her potions and spells while she got in touch
with the European Wiccan community. She had
looked forward to this year with an excitement I'd
never seen in her. For three long months she yam-
mered about how thrilling it was to be able to see Europe, and what an education I'd have going with her.
She even had the school district convinced that her
Ph.D. in education was good enough to tutor me for
the school year while I was dragged all over Eastern
and Western Europe.

Don't get me wrong; it's not like I love school or
anything, but at least there I fit in. Relatively. As long
as I didn't touch anyone. Most of the kids thought I
was just shy, which was fine with me. At least no one
thought I was a weirdo.

"I thought Absinthe said the last band ran off with
the money. If they're gone, how can they steal more
money?"

She fretted with her teacup, her spoon clinking
against the side as she stirred it a gazillion more times.
The sound of it set my teeth on edge. I buttered my
French toast and spread raspberry jam on it. "Peter
said this morning—this is in the strictest confidence,
Fran; you can't breathe a word of this to anyone, not

even Imogen—that the safe was rifled again sometime after Absinthe had put the evening's take in it. He
said he was going to have to call in the police, but I
don't see how that's going to do any good. Whoever
is stealing the money is very clever. He or she wouldn't
be so stupid as to leave their fingerprints on the safe.
Especially not if—"

She stopped and looked down at her tea as she
shook the spoon and set it on the table.

"If what?" I asked around a mouthful of French
toast.

Her light gray eyes lifted to meet mine. "If someone
is using their special powers to steal the money."

I swallowed. "Like who?"

"I don't know. Absinthe doesn't know. Peter
doesn't know. No one knows."

I made a half shrug, unwilling to admit that I would
be perfectly happy if the Faire went under and we
had to go home. "The police will probably find whoever it is."

"This is beyond the police, Fran. There's only one
person who can possibly determine who the thief is."

I didn't see it coming. I didn't see it at all, which
should prove once and for all that I don't have a single, solitary psychic cell in my body. At least not of the
precognitive kind. I stuffed another chunk of French
toast into my mouth. "Who's that?"

"You."

I choked, tears streaming from my eyes as I
wheezed, trying to get air into my lungs around the
big lump of French toast that was stuck in my throat.

"You're the only one who can find the thief, Fran."

"I'm not going to be able to do anything if I choke to death," I gasped.

She frowned. "I'm serious."

"So'm I!"

She handed me my mug of tea. "Franny, you have to do this. I know you don't like touching anyone—"

I wiped my streaming eyes with the back of my hand. "No."

"—but this is an emergency."

I shook my head, coughed, took a sip of tea, coughed again, and snarfed back the runny nose that always came with a near choking. "No!"

"I wouldn't ask you if it wasn't very important."

"It's not our problem! Absinthe and Peter can figure it out for themselves, or the police can."

"They can't, baby. If they could, they already would have. You have to help them."

"I don't have to do anything," I muttered to my half-eaten French toast.

"Please, Franny. Our whole future is at stake—"

"This isn't our future!" I shouted, slamming my hand down on the table so the mugs rattled. I was suddenly so mad I couldn't see straight. "Home is our future, not this freak show! I won't let you turn me into a monster like them! I just want to be normal like everyone else. You do understand normal, don't you? It's what you're not!"

Her eyes widened and I realized she was about to go into the "you're not a freak; you've been blessed, gifted with a skill that others would cherish" lecture. I knew it well; I heard it on the average of once a month, and at least once every couple of days after we arrived at the Faire, but I couldn't take it again. Not now. Not when I was so confused about Ben and everything.

"Where are you going?" she yelled as I jumped up from the table and grabbed my bag.

"Out."

"Francesca Marie—"

I slammed the door to the trailer on her words, jumping off the metal steps, holding my bag tight across my chest as I ran through the maze of trailers situated at the far end of the big meadow that held the Faire. Several of the Faire people said good morning to me, but I ignored all of them and settled down into a steady lope that I knew could last me a couple of miles. I ran through the trees ringing the meadow, down a small grassy slope, then onto the road that led to the town of Kapuvár.

Cars passed by on their way in and out of town, kicking up dust that swept over me, leaving my mouth and hair gritty. I slowed my lope to a trot, then a walk, trudging past field after field of cows, horses, goats, and some sheep. I rehashed the argument with my mother, changing it so I had all the good lines, my arguments so convincing she had to bow before my superior reasoning and admit that we belonged back home, not in the middle of Hungary. I muttered to myself as I passed a big white truck with wooden slatted sides, the kind they use to haul livestock. An old man who held a lead on a dirty gray horse was arguing with a tall, thin guy in expensive shoes. The tall guy kept looking around him as if he smelled something bad. A girl a few years younger than me was standing next to the fence, obviously trying not to cry.

I stopped because I like horses, and the old gray horse had lovely lines, a thickly curved neck, rounded haunch, deep chest, and big, big, soulful brown eyes.

"What's going on?" I asked the girl, forgetting for a moment that I wasn't back home where everyone spoke English. She turned and sniffed.

"It's Tesla, my *ópapi's*—grandfather's—horse. Milos is taking him away. You are American?"

"Yeah. Who's Milos?"

She pointed to the old man, who was now holding out his hand. The tall, thin guy was arguing with him as he doled out Hungarian forints (their dollars). "I study English in school. We are very good, yes? Milos, he is a . . ." She said something in Hungarian then.

"A what?" I asked.

She sniffled again. "He takes old horses, you know? And they make them into dog meat."

I stared in horror at the old man. "My God, that's horrible. Isn't that illegal or something? Why is that other guy letting him do it?"

"He is my uncle Tarvic. He says he can't afford to feed Tesla anymore, now that *ópapi* is dead, but it makes me so sad. Tesla is old, but he is special. My *ópapi* loved him more than all the other horses."

"Hey!" I yelled, scrabbling through my bag with one hand as I hurried through the gate toward the two men and the horse. The old horse nickered at me, nodding his head up and down as if he understood what I was going to do. I hoped he did, 'cause I sure didn't. "Hey, mister, I'll give you . . . uh . . . I have two hundred and forty dollars. U.S. cash. I'll give it to you for the horse."

The girl stood behind me, jabbering in Hungarian. I assumed she was translating for me, because the tall man turned and scowled at me. I dug out my wallet and waved the year's allowance that Dad had given me as a going-away present (or bribe, however you wanted to look at it). I held out the money. "Tell your uncle that I'll give him the money if he sells the horse to me, instead. That way he won't have to pay the knacker."

"Knacker?"

"Milos."

She turned and said something to her uncle. He eyed my cash with an avid gleam in his eye, but the old man started yelling at me, shoving me backward. I held the money out to Uncle Tarvic by the very tips of the ends. "Tell your uncle that I'm with the Faire just down the road, and that the horse will be fine; he'll be treated really well."

The girl hesitated. "He won't care; he doesn't like horses."

I made an exasperated noise. "Look, you can tell him whatever you want; just get him to take my money and give me the horse."

Milos the knacker was back to trying to shove me from the field, waving his hands around wildly. Tesla laid his ears back and snorted a warning at the gestures.

"You will treat him well? You will care for him?"

"Would I be willing to give up my whole year's allowance if I was going to be mean to him?" I asked. "Yes, I'll treat him really well. I've always wanted a horse, and since Peter has a horse trailer for the horse he uses in his magic act, hauling Tesla around won't be a problem. Please."

The girl nodded and turned back to her uncle, pleading with him. Evidently the sight of my money was too much, because Uncle Tarvic snatched his money back from Milos, and handed me the lead to the horse at the same time he grabbed the money from my hand. One finger of his brushed mine, but I jerked my hand back before I could pick up anything about him.

"*Köszönöm*," I said (Hungarian for "thank you"). "*Köszönöm.*"

I gave the lead a slight tug and the old horse started forward. I tried to remember on which side Soren walked when he led his dad's horse, Bruno, but Tesla evidently knew the ropes. He marched by my right side, heading for the road like he knew where he was going. Milos yelled and screamed a lot, but I only smiled as I led Tesla to the road, turning toward the way I had just come.

"What is your name?" the girl asked. Tesla stopped and looked back at her.

"Fran. What's yours?"

"Panna." She stepped up to Tesla, cupping her hands around his whiskery nose. He snorted on her hands. Her eyes were all weepy again, like she was going to cry. "He will be a very good horse, yes?"

"Yes, he will be a very good horse. If you like, you can come visit him while we're in town. We're going to be here three more days; then we go to Budapest."

She gave me a watery smile. "I will like that. Thank you, Fran. You are my friend."

"Sure thing. Well, come on, Tesla; we'd better get you back so I can start working on Mom."

"Working on Mom?" Panna asked.

"Nothing. I'll see you later?"

"As soon as I am able."

" 'Kay. See you."

I tugged on the lead and Tesla started walking amiably enough. I looked back once. Panna was getting in the car with her uncle. Milos was grinding the gears on his truck, driving in the opposite direction. I looked at Tesla. His long white eyelashes hid his eyes as he walked along next to me, periodically stopping to graze a particularly succulent-looking patch of grass.

I had a horse. An old horse. In the middle of Europe, where I had no home but a trailer, I bought a horse. I tried to think of a reason Mom shouldn't throw the hissy fit to end all hissy fits when she saw Tesla, but knew it was a lost cause. I had only one thing I could use as bargaining power. I sighed. Tesla, drowsing as we strolled along in the morning heat, bobbed his head and rolled an eye over to look at me. "You're going to cost me a whole lot more than money, horse. A whole lot more."

We walked the rest of the way to the Faire in silence, Tesla thinking horsey-type thoughts and paying no attention to the cars as they zoomed by us, me dreading the deal I was going to have to cut. I'd have to do what Mom wanted me to do.

I'd have to find out who the thief was.

Chapter Four

"Hey," Soren said, and set a bucket of water down beside me before plopping to the ground.

"Hey," I said back. "Thanks for the water. I'm sure Tesla will appreciate it when he's done stuffing his face."

We were sitting on a bank at the far edge of the meadow, beyond the area the cars used to park. Tesla was grazing happily away in the long shadows cast by the sun as it started to dip below the trees. I had spent most of the day just sitting there, watching him. He moved stiffly and slowly, but I didn't see any signs that he was deathly ill or ready to keel over any second, both of which Mom had suggested once she got over the shock of my arriving back at the trailer with a horse in tow.

"How did your mother take it?"

I shrugged and plucked a piece of tall grass from the bank. "She threw a hissy."

Soren's freckled nose scrunched up. "A hissy?"

48

"A hissy fit. She had kittens. A cow. You know—she ranted."

"Oh, ranted, yes, I'm familiar with ranted. My father rants always."

"Yeah, well, when your father rants, I bet flowers don't wilt and milk doesn't turn sour." That wasn't the worst of it. Once, when she got really mad at me because I went out to a club after she said I couldn't, every mirror in the house shattered. I was grounded for a month after that. Talk about your seven years' bad luck.

"No," Soren said thoughtfully. "Although once the doves all died."

Peter was one of the three magicians who practiced magic. He was the only one of the three who could do real magic, the kind you almost never see. His grand finale was turning a box of doves into Bruno, their horse, only that was an illusion, not real magic. The real magic . . . well, it gave you goose bumps to watch it.

"I suppose sour milk is better than dead birds."

Soren selected a big piece of grass, splitting it down the middle to make a reed out of it. He blew. It sounded wet and slobbery. I folded my blade of grass carefully, put it to my lips, and sent a stream of air through the narrow gap. A high, sharp squeal silenced the nearby bird chatter for a moment. Tesla lifted his head and looked at me. I tapped the water bucket with my toes. He wandered over and plunged his gray-black muzzle into it, drinking and snorting to himself.

"Miranda said you could keep him?"

I thought back to the hour-long argument we'd had once I returned. "Well . . . she said I'd have to get a job in the Faire to pay for his food and vet bills. And she said your dad had to okay him traveling with Bruno when we're on the road, and that a vet would have to look at him to make sure he didn't have a horrible horse disease. And I have to find him a home when it's time for us to go back to Oregon. But yes, she said I could keep him."

There was, of course, one other condition, the most important condition, the one that clinched the deal for me. I agreed to become Miss Touchy-Feely in an effort to figure out which one of the Faire employees (if any) was robbing Absinthe and Peter.

I frowned at Tesla, trying to decide if he was worth all the agony he was going to cost me. He pulled his nose out of the bucket, snuffled my feet, then lifted his head and blew horse snot and water all over my legs.

"You would have been a dog's dinner without me, Tesla. You just remember that little fact!" I grabbed a handful of long grass and wiped the snot and water off my right leg.

Soren sat resting his arms on his knees. "I saw Imogen this morning."

I threw away my handful of grass and got another one, glaring at Tesla as I wiped my other leg. "Yeah? So did I. She was getting a tan."

Soren tried to make a whistle out of another piece of grass, but it fell apart. He threw it at Tesla, who promptly ate it. "She said her brother is staying with her for a few days."

I knew that. Imogen had mentioned it to me the night before. It seemed they hadn't seen each other in a long time. I wondered how many hundreds of years "a long time" was to a vamp? I threw away my grass and stood up, walking over to pat Tesla's neck. "Yeah, I know."

Soren slid a sidelong glace at me. "I don't like him. He's too . . ." He said something in German.

"What?"

He waved his hands around. "Slippery. Slick. Fast. I don't think he is nice."

"Really?" I held on to Tesla's halter and stroked my hand down his lovely curved chest. It was thick with muscles, even at his age. He turned his head and nuzzled my hand. I scratched his ears for a minute, then slid my hand under his mane and ran it down his neck, enjoying the feeling of warm horse beneath my fingertips. "I like him. He's— What the heck?"

I pushed aside a dirty length of mane and looked at the spot where Tesla's shoulder met his neck. Nothing looked different—it was all dirty gray horse hair—but running my fingers lightly along his upper left shoulder, I felt something, a thickening, like a big scar. "He must have hurt himself a long time ago," I said to myself.

"Who, Benedikt?"

"No, Tesla. Touch him here. What do you feel?"

Soren limped over and ran his hand over the horse's shoulder. "Horse."

"Try again."

Soren did, made a face, and wiped his hand on his shorts. "Sweaty horse. About Benedikt—"

I tipped the water over with my foot. Soren jumped back out of the way of the creeping puddle. I scooped the bucket up and handed it to him, clipping the lead onto Tesla's halter. "Come on, I want to give him a bath. You can help before the evening rush starts. The vet is going to see him tomorrow, so he has to look healthy."

Soren frowned, but followed me as I led Tesla across the grassy parking area. "You're avoiding the subject."

"Yeah, I know. I'm doing pretty good at it, too, huh?"

He sighed one of those dramatic sighs that guys who are fifteen sigh. "I warned you. When you come crying to me that he did something terrible to you, don't tell me I didn't warn you."

I smiled and nudged him with my elbow. "Deal."

I'll say this for Soren—he might be jealous of Ben's very cool motorcycle (and working on Mom to let me go for a ride on it was next on my list), but he was willing to let it go in order to show me how to take care of a horse. Bruno, Peter's flashy Andalusian, looked positively sparkly white compared to Tesla's dingy gray, but an hour later, after having soaped him up and rinsed him off (much to Tesla's delight—I swear that horse positively moaned with happiness when Soren produced a curry comb), he looked less gray and more like a true white. I spent another half hour combing out his mane and tail, so he was looking pretty spiffy by the time Peter stopped to check Tesla's feet and mouth.

"He's old," Peter said as he peered into Tesla's open mouth. "Probably twenty, twenty-five years. But he looks in fairly good shape." He let go of the horse's lips and patted him on the neck. Tesla arched it and did a stiff little prance-in-place move. Peter laughed. "Nice old boy. He should cause us no trouble. Your mother says you will work to pay for his feed, true?"

"True." I nodded, feeling all warm and fuzzy because Tesla was showing off. The big galoot. "I can do concessions, or tickets, or move stuff, or—"

Peter shook his head. "You will learn the palm reading from Imogen. Your mother tells me you will be good at it, and Imogen wishes to read the runes only. You will learn from her. I will pay you in feed for Tesla while you learn; then you will get real wages, yes?"

My stomach wadded up into a little ball at the thought of reading people's palms. That would mean I'd have to touch them! Sneaky, sneaky Mom. She had been trying for the last couple of years to get me to do readings for people. Now she had me right where she wanted me.

Man, you buy one horse and all of a sudden your life goes all complicated! I patted Tesla, thinking that before that morning, everything was crystal-clear to me—more than anything, I wanted to go back home. Of course, there was Ben . . . but there was nothing to stop him from going to Oregon, was there?

Tesla, however, was another subject. I was pretty sure I couldn't take him home with me; that would be way too expensive. So that meant either I had to stay and give in to my mother's evil plan to make me one of Them, or I could stay and just refuse to do anything, and mope and pout until everyone got sick of me and sent me back to live with my dad (which, to be honest, wasn't looking that good, what with the new trophy wife in the picture), or I could give up Tesla and make the best of things.

I looked at Tesla. He looked back at me with his big, liquid brown eyes. There was nothing wrong with him; he was just old. Did he deserve to be chopped up into dog food just because I didn't want to do a little investigating and some stupid palm reading?

I sighed again (I really have to stop; it's getting to be a bad habit), and nodded at Peter. "All right. I'll let Imogen teach me to read palms." On my own terms— I'd wear my gloves.

"Good, good. Soren, come with me; I have much work for you. . . ."

They hurried off to the little trailer that served as an office. The generator behind the main tent hummed, then snapped into life, the big lights running down either side of the fairway buzzing on one after the other. Shadows sprang up, their edges crisp and clear in the bright blue-white light that flooded the ground, turning the green grass silvery black. Tesla whinnied, pawing the ground with one hoof as I ran the brush over him one last time.

"Found a new friend, have you?"

Ben's voice curled alongside me, almost as if it were actually touching my skin. I looked over Tesla's back. "Yep. I bought him earlier today. He's mine."

"You bought him?" Ben's black eyebrows rose as he approached us. Tesla snorted and tossed his head up and down, trying to pull away from where I had tied him to the bumper of Peter's bus. "You bought a horse. A little souvenir of Hungary?"

"Something like that."

Ben put a hand out and caught Tesla's halter, murmuring soothing things as he stroked the horse's head, calming him down.

"Don't tell me: Dark Ones have a special ability to calm horses?"

He grinned that infectious grin that made me want to smile back. "Nothing so exciting. I just happen to like horses. What's his name?"

"Tesla."

"Hmm." Ben stroked Tesla's neck just as I had done. I bent over to brush his legs, and when I stood up, Ben was frowning at the horse's shoulder.

"There's a scar there," I pointed out to him.

"Yes, I noticed," Ben said. His fingers traced out the letter P, two Xs, and beneath it, a wavy line.

"What's that?" I asked. Ben looked up at me. "The symbols you were drawing. Were you warding him?"

A slow smile spread across his face. "What do you know about wards?"

I put the brush back into the bucket and stepped back from Tesla. He looked pretty good, if I did say so myself. "Not a lot. Imogen said she'd show me how to draw them sometime, but she's always so busy. Did you ward Tesla?"

"No," Ben said. "Where did you get him?"

I explained my morning's adventure, leaving out all

the stuff about Mom and my promise to help find the thief. He wasn't going to be around long enough for that to matter to him.

"You know nothing about where the girl's grandfather got him?"

"Nope."

"Not even his name?"

"Tesla's?"

"The grandfather's."

I shook my head. "Nope. Is it important? Should I have gotten a receipt? My mother says I should have, that someone could claim I stole him, but I have Panna as a witness."

"I don't think a receipt would tell you anything," Ben said slowly, still stroking Tesla. He traced something on the horse's cheek. "If you like, I can look into finding out where he originated."

Tesla turned and bumped me with his head. I peeled off my gloves and scratched behind his ears. "Why?"

Ben raised an eyebrow. He was looking just as nummy as he had the night before, although this time he had on black pants and a bloodred shirt that looked soft and shimmery, like it was silk. He had two little black stone earrings in his left ear, and a diamond in his right. We are talking *major* cool, here. "Do you always ask *why* when someone offers to do you a favor?"

"Sometimes. If I think the favor is going to cost me something."

He smiled again. "This will cost you."

I walked around behind Tesla, being sure to stay

clear of his back legs just in case he was a kicker.
"How much? I spent all my money on him."

"Think you can convince your mother to give you
permission to come on a ride with me?"

I sucked in my breath. "On your bike?" He nodded,
his fingers still gently stroking Tesla's neck. "That's an
awfully strange payment. How about we just go on
the ride and not worry about the okay?"

"No." He shook his head and held out his hand for
me. "You must get permission or there will be no
ride."

I hesitated, chewing my lip as I looked at it. It was
just a hand, just five fingers and a palm. I had touched
him before, and I had been okay. There was no reason
not to trust him now. I took a step closer to him,
stretching out my arm, my hand poised over his.

I swear the air between our hands got hot.

"Are you turned off?" I asked.

He didn't say anything, just looked at me with pitch-
black eyes. I let two of my fingers droop down to
touch him.

It was just a hand.

"You never have anything to fear from me," he said
softly, his thumb rubbing the back of my hand. "If you
ever find yourself in trouble, I will help you. Without
any questions."

"And all I have to do is save your soul in return?" I
asked, pulling my hand out of his.

He shook his head. "I ask nothing of you. I never
will, Fran."

I pretended my arm itched, and scratched at it just

to break the moment. His unblinking gaze made me uncomfortable, leaving me very aware that he was a gorgeous guy in a red silk shirt and I was a big lump of a girl in a dirty pair of jeans and a sweaty T-shirt.

I picked up the bucket of grooming tools and turned toward the horse trailer, saying over my shoulder, "I'll ask my mom about the ride in the morning. She's not too happy with me tonight. At least she won't be until I start—" I stopped. It was just so easy to talk to Ben, I forgot that I didn't need to blab every thought I had to him.

"Until you start what?"

He followed me around to the front of the horse trailer, where Soren told me they kept Bruno's grain. I measured out the amount he'd mentioned, dumping it into a bucket. "Here, you carry this."

Ben took the bucket, watching as I frowned at a bale of hay. "How much is a flake? Soren just said a flake. Half, do you think?"

"No, look, you can see the natural divisions in the bale. That's a flake."

"How do you know so much about horses?"

He did a half smile. "I told you—you're not the only one who likes them."

"Oh. Have you had one? I mean, like, long ago? You know, when everyone had horses?" He looked so normal (an understatement if there ever was one) that it was hard to remember that he was walking around a couple of centuries ago, before they had cars, before they had electricity, before stuff like penicillin and anesthetic. I wanted to ask him about a gazillion questions, but figured that would have to wait.

"Yeah, I've had horses."

"I guess you would have to, huh? Did you take care of them yourself?"

His half smile got a bit quirkier. "No. I had grooms."

"Grooms? Like servants?"

He nodded.

I just stood there with my mouth hanging open like a big dumb girl. "Are you royalty or something?"

He laughed and chucked me under the chin, just like you do to a little kid. "No, I'm not royalty, Fran. You don't have to look so appalled."

I turned away, yelling at myself for being such a boob as I pulled loose a chunk about six inches wide and carried it over to the opposite side of the trailer, where Bruno was munching down on his dinner. Ben set the bucket down, then went and fetched a second with water for the horses while I brought Tesla over and tied him on a long lead to the trailer. "Din-dins! Bon appetit."

"Fran? What is it you have to start?"

I turned and faced Ben. Just what I needed in my life, a vamp with a one-track mind. "It's nothing, okay? Just a little project I have to do for my mother. Something I had to agree to in order to keep Tesla. So you can stop prying and leave me alone."

Sometimes I'd like to kick myself. Other times I just want to step out of my skin, point to my body, and say, "I'm not with her." This was one of the times when I wanted to do both.

"Sorry," Ben said, and without giving me anything more than a quick glance, he turned around and walked off.

Crap, crap, and double crap! Could I be any more stupid? The cutest guy in the whole universe—okay, he's a bloodsucker, but no one's perfect—and I have to snap at him until he goes off to talk to smaller, shorter, prettier girls, girls he doesn't have to pretend to like just because they can save his soul.

"My life totally sucks," I told Tesla. He twitched his tail aside and pooped. "Thank you. I *so* needed that."

I scooped the horse poop out of the way, made sure Tesla was okay for a while, then figured, as long as I was miserable and unhappy and depressed, I might as well be *really* miserable and unhappy and depressed.

Fran Getti, the Nancy Drew of the twenty-first century.

Not!

Chapter Five

"Miranda says you have agreed to find the thief who steals our money. She vill not tell me how it is you are to do this. I am naturally curious. You vill tell me now." Absinthe set her overnight bag down next to her trailer, and turned to bark something in German to Karl, who had picked her up from the train station. Imogen says that Karl is Absinthe's boy toy, but I have a hard time believing that. It isn't that Absinthe is ugly, but her spiky pink hair doesn't quite go with the hard jaw and mean little eyes.

Her German accent was a lot heavier than Peter's and Soren's, but even so, when she turned her washed-out pale-blue eyes on you, you got her meaning. She was also a mind reader, a fact that made me really nervous around her. Much as I disliked Ben marching in and rifling through my mind, at least I trusted him. To a certain extent. Absinthe I didn't trust farther than I could spit. "Um . . . actually, I don't think I will tell you. Mom didn't say that was part of the bargain."

"Bargain?" Absinthe spun around and narrowed her eyes at me. It was late morning, and she'd just returned from her trip to Germany to find a replacement band. Most of the Faire people were just waking up, but I figured I'd get a start on my new role as detective, and fire up the investigation . . . such as it was. "Vat bargain is this?"

"The bargain that says I get to keep my horse if I help you. I figured the first thing I need to do is talk to you about the thefts, and maybe see the safe and stuff like that."

She gave me another narrow-eyed look, then turned and entered the trailer. I assumed I was supposed to follow, and climbed up after her. I figured the inside of the trailer would look like the outside (pink and green, remember?)—in other words, garish—but it was surprisingly uncluttered. There was an awful lot of that shade of tan called taupe, but the little couch, two chairs, and tiny table that made up the main part of the trailer were actually pretty tasteful. Absinthe set her overnight bag down on the table and waved at the curved bank of the couch.

"This is the safe. As you can see, it is a good safe, very reliable, *ja?* In the morning ven I come awake, I open the safe to take out the money for food, but there was no money, only newspaper. It was that Josef, in the band, you know? *Verdammter Schweinehund!* He is trying to ruin us!"

I squatted down in front of the safe. It was big, about two feet high, made of white-painted metal, with the usual spin dial thingy on the front, a metal handle to open it, and not a lot else. I prodded it with my toe. It probably weighed a couple of hundred pounds.

"Who has the combination to the safe?"

"Peter and I do." She shook out her linen jacket and hung it up in a tiny closet.

"No one else?"

"Of course not; do you take us for the fools?"

I tried to think of what I would do if I wanted to break into the safe. "Um . . . when do you normally open it?"

She grabbed her bag and brushed past me, opening the door behind me to her bedroom. "In the morning, to pay out such money as ve need to Elvis and Kurt for purchasing food and anything ve need for the shows."

Kurt was Karl's brother. Another boy toy, or so Imogen said.

"And you put money into it at night?"

"I do it, *ja*. I put it in a bag like this, you see?" She held up an empty black money bag, the kind with a zipper and a lock on the end. "The money goes in once ven I count up the ticket sales, and also after the fair closes, ven all the money comes from the employees."

The Faire contract called for all the performers to split their takes with Peter and Absinthe. In return they had their travel expenses paid, and were guaranteed a minimum amount each month.

"Ven I look in the morning, fffft! The money is gone, and the bag is filled vith newspaper."

I chewed on my lip as I watched Absinthe unzip her travel bag. I didn't want her to see me touching the safe—if she knew about my little curse, she'd demand

I be put to work as the resident Teen Freak. With my back to her, I peeled off the gloves from my right hand and reached for the safe handle. With Absinthe liable to finish putting away her stuff any second, I didn't have time to brace myself for the onslaught of images. I just grabbed the handle and hoped for the best.

It was awful. Worse than I thought. At least seven different people had touched the safe in the last few weeks: Absinthe and Peter were the strongest, but I could also feel Karl, Elvis, Soren, even Imogen and my mom had touched the safe at some time or another. Inanimate objects can't hold on to memories the way people do, but if someone was feeling a very strong emotion when he or she touched it, sometimes that was imprinted onto the object.

Indecision and frustration were there on the safe handle, but the overwhelming feeling, the emotion that swamped my mind was a cold, quiet desperation, the kind of desperation that makes your palms prick with sweat. One of the people who'd touched the safe was emotionally in a state so bad that touching the memory of it now left me slightly sick to my stomach.

I pulled my hand away, but didn't have time to get the glove back on before Absinthe popped into the room. "I am not seeing how you can help us if you vill not tell me how you work. Do you read the minds, eh? Can you see someone's guilt in their aura? Are you a human . . . what do you call it . . . lie detector?"

I gave her a feeble smile and shoved my bare hand behind my back, slowly backing down the narrow aisle of the trailer so she wouldn't see it. "None of that, sorry. Mom just thinks I can help. I read a lot of Agatha Christies."

Absinthe crossed her arms and glared at me. "I don't think that is at all the amusing. How vill you help us now?"

I reached for the door with my gloved hand, still keeping my back away from her. "I'll probably talk to everyone and see if anyone has noticed anything "

"Bah!" She threw her hands in the air in a gesture of annoyance. "Useless, that is useless. I have questioned everyone and no one sees anything, no one notices anything wrong. This is a vaste of my time."

I let one shoulder twitch in a half a shrug. "Yeah, well, I made a bargain with my mother, and I'll stick to it." *No matter how much it destroys me*, I added silently. "I'll let you know if I find out anything."

Absinthe thinned her lips at me, her eyes glittering brightly. I stood with one foot on the step, one in the trailer, suddenly unable to move, locked into place by that look. My scalp tingled as I realized what she was doing. I could feel her nudging against my consciousness, trying to find a way into my mind. I wanted to yell at her to stay out of my head, but I felt as if I were caught in a big vat of molasses, as if everything going on around me had been switched into slow motion. Panic, dark and cold, gripped me as I could feel her sliding around me, surrounding me, suffocating me. She was going to get in, and then she'd know everything about me! I couldn't breathe; my lungs couldn't get any air in them. I felt squashed flat by her power, by her ability to just push aside my feeble resistance and march into my head. Everything started to go gray as I was swept up in wave of dizziness.

No! my brain shrieked.

Fran?

Warmth filled me, eased the stranglehold Absinthe held on me, allowed my lungs to expand and suck in much-needed air. I clutched at the warmth. *Ben?*

Is something wrong? He sounded sleepy, a warm, comfortable sleepy, as if he were snuggled down in a warm bed on a cold winter morning. The touch of his mind on mine was reassuring, pushing away the gray dizziness, blanketing me in security.

Absinthe is trying to get into my mind. She'll find out about me, about you, too.

She already knows about me. Don't worry; she won't get in. Imagine yourself in a sealed chamber, with no way in and no way out. Just you. Imagine yourself in that, and she won't be able to get into your mind.

I took a deep breath, my eyes still on Absinthe's as she made a big push at my mind. My knees almost buckled under the attack. *Ben!*

Think of the sealed room, Fran. His voice was so soothing, so filled with confidence, it helped push some of the black panic away. I pictured a room made of stainless steel, all rounded corners, the seams of which were welded together. There wasn't a crack, wasn't a space anywhere that anything could get in or out. It was absolutely airtight, sealed, and I stood in the middle of it.

Absinthe's hold on me snapped just as if I severed a

taut rope. She snarled in German, but I didn't wait around to see what else she had to say. I babbled something about seeing her later, and ran for my life.

Ben?

He didn't answer. I couldn't feel him, either. I couldn't feel anything, not one single thing. There was just me in my brain. *Ben, are you angry because I woke you up? I'm sorry if you are, but I wanted to let you know that your idea worked. Absinthe didn't get into my head. Everything's okay now. Um. Unless you're mad at me, and then I guess everything is not okay.*

Nothing. *Nada.* Not one blessed thing. He didn't even think angry at me, the way he could think a smile.

I sighed and looked around. There're not a lot of places to hide when you're living in a big, open, grassy meadow with a bunch of tents and a cluster of trailers. I had no idea where I was going, but weaved through the trailers until I arrived at one with Norse symbols painted in gold and black. I knocked on the door as I turned the handle and slid through the door, glancing over my shoulder to make sure that no one saw me going into Imogen's trailer. "Imogen? You up? I really need to talk to you."

The shades were up, sunlight slanting into the trailer, highlighting the remains of a bagel on the tiny little table, so I gathered Imogen was up and about.

"You getting dressed?" I headed for the closed door to her bedroom. "Listen, I have a question for you— Ohmigosh!"

It wasn't Imogen in the bedroom; it was Ben. With a bare chest. Sitting up in Imogen's bed with a sleepy, surprised look on his face.

Until I moved and a tendril of sunlight snaked past me into the room, falling on his bare arm. He yelped and jerked the blanket up, squinting at me.

"I'm so sorry!" I tried to move to block the sunlight, but more came in around the other side of me. "Geez, I'm sorry, I can't . . . stupid sun . . ."

"Get in and close the door," he snapped. I jumped into the room and slammed the door shut behind me.

That was when I realized that I was standing in a tiny little dimly lit bedroom with a naked vampire who looked really, really mad.

He clicked the bedside light on, pushing the blanket down to look at his arm. At the sight of the blisters that streaked up his arm I forgot all about being embarrassed that he was naked. "Did I do that? Oh, Ben, I'm so sorry. What should I . . . Ice, that's what you put on a burn."

"Don't open that door again!" he yelled just as I was about to go hunt for ice. "I don't need anything; it will be all right."

"Don't be stupid; those are like third . . . degree . . . wow." Ben stroked his burned arm. With each pass of his hand, the blisters lessened until all that remained were faintly red angry marks on his nummy tan skin. "That's amazing! You're a healer!"

"Not really." He slumped back against the wall. "I have limited regenerative powers. The weaker I am, the less I am able to heal."

"Weak?" I reached out to touch his arm, realized I

had my gloves on, and yanked them off. The second my fingers touched his skin I was filled with hunger, gnawing at me, biting me with sharp, painful stabs, a need building within me to take what I needed, to subdue that animal that growled within. I jerked my fingers back and stared at Ben. "You're hungry. Is that what you meant by weak?"

He ran his hand through his hair and looked peeved. "Yes. Is there a reason you're here?"

I stared at him, unable to look away. Okay, so I was looking a lot at his bare chest, but still, even with drooling over that, I couldn't help but wonder how he could have so much pain locked inside him, yet seem so normal on the outside. "I was looking for Imogen."

"She's not here."

"Yeah, I figured that out. How come you're hungry? I mean, why aren't you . . . *you know* . . . feeding?"

"I don't like fast food," he said. I blinked. He sighed. "That was a joke. It's not as easy as just picking a person out of a crowd and guzzling, Fran. I have to be careful about whom I chose."

"Oh, because of disease and stuff? HIV?"

"No, I'm immune to disease. I'm referring to the fact that most people would notice if their wife or sister or daughter suddenly showed up woozy and suffering from a significant blood loss. It takes longer to find several people who can provide me the amount of blood I need without leaving them with a noticeable loss."

"Huh. I hadn't thought of that." I bit my lip and eyed his arm. The red marks still looked like they hurt, and I knew what sort of pain he held inside him. Since I had caused him pain, I figured it was up to me to sacrifice a little blood. Besides, there was something almost . . . *intriguing* about the thought of giving him my blood. "How about me?"

His eyebrows went up. "What?"

"You could have a little snack."

"Snack?" He looked like I had a boob sprouting out of my forehead.

"Yeah, you know, bite. Nibble. *Sink fang.* Not enough to make me woozy, but enough to tide you over until you can find someone else to . . . um . . . eat."

Just in case you're wondering, this officially qualified as the strangest conversation I'd ever had.

Ben ran his hand through his hair again. I liked the way his arm muscles moved, but I tried not to let him see me admiring them. I'm really not looking for a boyfriend. Okay, the truth is, I wouldn't know what to do with one if I had him, but I decided it was better not to dwell on that. "Fran, I can't have your blood."

"You can't?" Because he was mad at me? So mad he would rather sit there so hungry it hurt rather than sip a little Fran? "Oh. Okay. No problem. Forget I mentioned it."

He rubbed his face. "It's not because I don't want to—there's nothing I'd like more than to bind us together—but that's exactly what it would mean: we would be bound together for the rest of our lives, which, incidentally, would be measured in centuries rather than decades."

I stood at the door, part of me wanting to run screaming from the room, the other part wanting to stay and talk to him. He *looked* so normal. . . . "It would?"

He sighed and pulled the blanket up his chest a bit. "A Dark One who joins with his Beloved by taking her blood cannot feed from anyone else. They are bound to each other, together, for eternity, giving each other life."

"Oh, you mean you'd have to . . ." I made claw fingers and gestured toward my neck with them.

He nodded.

"Right, so snacking is out. I like you and all, but I don't think I want to spend eternity with you. You don't . . . uh . . . mind me saying that, do you? You're not still mad at me?"

He frowned. He even frowned cute. Maybe I should rethink this whole no boyfriend thing. "I'm not mad at you, Fran. Why would you think I was?"

I waved a hand around vaguely. "You didn't answer me earlier, and I woke you up and all. . . ."

"I didn't answer you?"

"Yeah, after I left Absinthe, I did the weirdo psychic mind-meld thingy with you to thank you, but you didn't answer. I figured you were PO'd at me."

He yawned into his hand. "Do it now."

"Huh?"

"Try the weirdo psychic mind-meld thingy now."

"Ah. *Like this?*

He just looked at me.

Hellooooooooo? Ben? Anyone in there?

"Well?"

"You're not answering. If you're not going to answer you could at least have voice mail or something."

One corner of his mouth quirked up. "Fran, what was the last thing you did before you left Absinthe?"

I gave him moue-lips. "You know, you told me to do it! I imagined I was in a sealed room where nothing could get into my mind."

"And nothing could get out?"

I blinked at him for a second, then grinned. "Oh. I didn't think of that. How do I unseal my mind?"

"You imagined yourself protected in the room; just visualize that protection gone."

I chewed on my lip. "Will I be able to get it back again? I don't think Absinthe is one to give up too easily. In fact, I don't know what's stopping her from reading everyone's mind who works here." And incidentally figuring out for herself who stole the money.

He yawned again. "You can protect yourself whenever you need to. Everyone can; Absinthe can't read anyone's mind who has protected it. The first thing someone with a psychic ability learns is how to protect their mind from invasion. Didn't your mother teach you that?"

"Um . . . no." I pictured myself opening a door to the stainless-steel room and stepping outside it. *Thanks, Ben.*

"You're welcome. Is there anything else?"

"No. I'm sorry I woke you, twice. And sorry about the arm. And the whole Beloved thing. I don't imagine you're terribly happy about it, either."

His eyes glittered blackly at me as he pulled the blanket up to his neck.

"Will you take me for a ride tonight? Mom says I

can as long as I'm back by ten. I know that doesn't give you a lot of time after the sun goes down, but—"

"I'll see you at nine."

I nodded and waited until he pulled the blanket over his head before opening the door. I left a note for Imogen on her table, then hurried out, feeling pretty good about things. Ben wasn't mad at me, and had shown me how to beat Absinthe at her own game. Mom was in a relatively happy mood with me after I agreed to do what she wanted. Tesla looked happier at his new life—the vet had given him a clean bill of health—and he even did his funny little dance-in-place step when Soren and I led him and Bruno out and put chain hobbles around their front feet so they could graze loose in the meadow without running off.

Sure, I still had all that Nancy Drewing to do, but all in all, life was starting to look up.

Chapter Six

My life sucks bullfrogs. No, seriously, I mean it.

Oh, okay, maybe it's not *that* bad. But if you found yourself having to talk to a guy who not only looked like Elvis Presley, and sounded like Elvis Presley, but who actually thought he *was* Elvis Presley, wouldn't your day be a bit on the bullfrog-sucking side? Yeah. I thought so.

"Hey, there, little lady. What can the big man do for you, uh-huh?"

See? Sucky.

"Hi, Elvis. I wondered if I could talk to you for a couple of minutes."

He did a little hip shake as he combed his big black 'do in front of the floor mirror he always set up outside of his trailer. Elvis was thin, a little shorter than me, and had lots and lots of thick black hair that he greased back into a puffy-fronted fifties hairdo. I can't believe guys actually wore their hair like that, but mom says her dad used to, which is going to make me a little weird about Grandpa when I see him again.

"Sure ya can." He did another hip shake. Elvis is very big on his hip shakes. "Pull up a chair and we'll jaw awhile."

"I want you to tell me a little bit about demons."

He stopped in mid–hip shake, and turned around to look at me. "Demons? Now what would a little filly like you want with a big, bad ol' demon?"

Elvis is the resident demonologist. He claims he doesn't actually raise them (which I guess is major bad news), but Mom says there's something about his aura she doesn't trust. Technically Elvis is supposed to counsel people who think they're being plagued by a demon, and provide protective talismans against further demon attacks. I guess he does a roaring trade among businessmen.

"Well, I want to know what sort of things a demon can do for you. If you raised one, that is."

Elvis scowled and turned back to the mirror. "Your mama tell you to ask me that?"

"No, she doesn't know I'm talking to you. In fact, she'd be pretty ticked off if she knew I was. She doesn't like anything to do with the dark powers."

He snorted and stepped back to admire himself in the mirror. "Nothin' wrong with the dark powers as long as you know how to handle them." He turned and pointed his comb at me. "Demons ain't for little girls to play with, though. It takes a strong person to handle 'em."

I only *just* kept from rolling my eyes at the "little girl" comment. I'm three inches taller than him! "Can you make them do whatever you want?"

Elvis slipped on a leather jacket despite the fact that

it was warm out. He does a trick during Kurt and Karl's Malevolent Magick show where they materialize him in full Elvis regalia right into a glass box on the middle of the stage. Soren says he thinks it's an illusion, not real magic, but I can't figure out how they do it if it's not real. "Demons? Course you can, assuming you're strong enough. If you aren't, you'll be demon chow."

He made snapping sounds like he was eating someone up.

"Are there any limits to what you can get a demon to do?"

"Limits?" He lit a cigarette and offered me one. I shook my head. "What kind of limits?"

"Like . . . can they go through walls? Say, into the box that you materialize into?"

He snorted and blew smoke out his nose (I hate that). "Honey, there ain't nothin' that can keep a demon out from someplace it wants into, 'cept if you were to draw a bunch of wards. Or if the walls were made of steel. They *hate* steel. Burns 'em."

"Oh. Okay. Well, thanks a lot, Elvis. I'd better be on my way. Have to help Mom set up."

"You're not planning on raisin' yourself a demon, now, are you?"

I held up my hand, oath style. "Nope. Wouldn't know how if I wanted to."

"Good. Demons should be left to those who know how to handle 'em." He turned to give himself one last look in the mirror. I reached out with my left hand (which just had the lace glove on, no latex underneath it) and gently touched his back. Latex and animal hide were the only things that could tamp down on my ability to feel things when I touched people, but I really hated the thought of filling my mind with Elvis. I was sure the dimmed version would tell me enough.

I snatched my hand back, smiling wildly as he turned around toward me. "Thanks! See you later."

Or never, if I got my wish. I had the worst desire to go take a shower, to wash out of my mind the lewd images and thoughts about Imogen that filled Elvis's. If they had such a thing as brain shampoo, I'd be buying a truckload of it.

"What a pervert," I said as I headed toward Imogen's tent. I was going to be sure to tell her to watch out for him—the things he was thinking about her just weren't healthy. "But at least he's a pervert who couldn't get a demon to steal the money for him. Not from a steel-lined safe."

Imogen's tent was empty. She'd been gone all day, probably shopping in town (she loved to shop), but it wasn't like her to be away so close to opening. I glanced across the meadow. I'd moved Tesla to the small section behind the portable toilets so he could graze out of the way of the Fairegoers. Soren was brushing Bruno, getting him ready for his appearance in Peter's magic act. The sun was still barely visible through the trees, long amber and pink fingers stretching across a deepening sky. In another half hour it would be dark, and the GothFaire would spring to life. Hundreds of people would tramp through the Faire, laughing, shrieking, having body parts pierced, communicating with their dead loved ones, playing with torture devices . . . you know, the usual evening out.

I went over the mental list of people who had touched the safe. Elvis, my prime suspect, was a no-go. Imogen and Mom, I was sure, were just coincidence. Peter had no reason to rob himself (motive, the detectives call it), and Soren probably also had a legitimate reason to be putting something into the safe. Which left Karl.

I looked down the long center aisle to where Kurt and Karl were wheeling their props into the main tent. I stopped by one of the booths to get a wurst and a big pretzel, scarfing the wurst down as I walked toward the main tent.

"Hey, Soren," I said, pausing by the horse trailer. He was rubbing shiny stuff onto Bruno's hooves to make them pretty. I held out the pretzel.

"Thanks," he said, wiping his hands onto his rumpled shorts before taking it. "You want me to feed Tesla with Bruno?"

I licked the last of the wurst juice off my fingers, frowning just a little. "That would be really nice of you, but you don't have to do it."

He grinned and chomped off a big bite of pretzel.

I was instantly suspicious. "Okay, how come you're being nice?"

He glanced around, his grin deepening. "*Tante* told me you're supposed to be figuring out who has been stealing the money. I thought you might be *on the case.*"

"You watch way too much American TV," I said, and pulled on both sets of my gloves. "Speaking of that, have you noticed anything suspicious about the safe?"

"Suspicious?" Little bits of dough flew out as he

talked around his mouthful of pretzel. "What is suspicious about a safe?"

I did a little sideways head bob. "I don't know . . . someone hanging around it who shouldn't be, someone in the trailer when your aunt or dad puts money away, anyone who knows the combination, that sort of thing."

He looked around quickly, then leaned in, tapping his chest. "I know the combination."

I raised my eyebrows. "You do?"

"Yes, Papa wrote it down on a piece of paper because he was always forgetting it. He left the paper in the tent one day. I picked it up."

My mouth hung open just a little bit until I realized that and got a grip on myself. "You mean to say that your dad left the combination to the safe out in the open where anyone could see it?"

"Not out in the open, no. It was in the tent a few weeks ago, when we were in Stuttgart, remember? It was on the dove case with some notes about towns we were going to. The only people who could have seen it were—"

"Anyone connected with the Faire, and that includes the band who ran out in the night. Jeezumcrow, Soren, anyone could be opening the safe! Did you tell Peter that you found the combination?"

He shook his head and stuffed the last of the pretzel into his mouth. "I put it back in the desk, so he wouldn't know it was gone. But I saw the number on it. I remember."

I looked at him, really looked, the way Mom says you should look at people, to see past their outer surface and into their soul. I've never been able to see into souls, but she says it just takes patience and practice. I tried now. I cleared my mind of all the suspicions and worries and other stuff that was polluting my thoughts, and looked at Soren.

I saw nothing. So much for Mom's way.

"Cow cookies," I snarled, and peeled off my gloves, touching his arm. He looked surprised at that, but I didn't pay attention, I was too busy trying to beat off all the things going on in his mind. Images of his dad smiling and laughing battled with Peter snapping at him, telling him he wasn't trying, that he would never be anything but an illusionist if he didn't put his mind to his work. There were also quick flashes of Absinthe yelling at Peter, pleasurable moments of time when Soren worked with the animals, taking care of Bruno, feeding the doves, even petting Davide. Most surprising of all, there were also images of me in his mind, confusing images that didn't make any sense because they were overlaid with a mixture of frustration and pleasure.

There was nothing of the quiet desperation I felt on the safe, however.

"Are you okay? You look funny, like you're mad and happy at the same time."

I pulled my hand from his arm and gave him a half smile. "Yeah, I'm okay. Just trying something."

He looked interested. "An experiment? A detective experiment?" His eyes opened wide. "Am I a . . . a . . . what did they call it . . . a perp?"

"Man, you really *are* watching too much American

TV." I laughed, glad for a chance to shake the creepy feeling I always got when I peeked into people's minds. "No, you're not a perp. Did you mean what you said?"

He dug through a canvas satchel and pulled out two apples, offering me one. I shook my head. "About what?"

"About bringing Tesla in for me. I have something to do at nine, so if you wouldn't mind doing it, I'd really appreciate it."

He leaned close and asked in a hoarse whisper, "Are you going to be giving everyone the third degree?"

I whapped him on the arm with my elbow. "No, stupid, I'm . . . I'm going to meet . . . I'm going to . . . um . . ."

He just looked at me as I stumbled over my tongue.

"Ben's going to take me for a motorcycle ride, that's all. It's nothing, really."

He froze, the apple halfway to his mouth as his eyes got small. "You've got a date with Benedikt?"

"It's not a date; it's just a ride on his motorcycle."

Soren blinked. "Did Miranda say you could go? I thought you said she didn't want you being with him?"

"She did, but she changed her mind, and before you say anything else, you can just stop, because it's not what you think."

"You don't know what I'm thinking," he said quietly.

"You'd be surprised," I muttered. "Thanks for taking care of Tesla tonight. I owe you. I'll see you later, 'kay?"

I hurried off before he could say anything else. It occurred to me that although I wasn't going on a date or anything, I didn't want Ben to see me in the same old grubby tee and jeans that Tesla had slobbered over. Mom was still in the trailer, just getting ready to go do her witch stuff. She stayed long enough to give me yet another lecture about going out with Ben (she insisted on thinking of this as a date, which it clearly wasn't, but no one else but me seemed to realize that), pressing her most powerful amulet into my hand.

"Let me see you put it on."

"Mom! I don't need it. Ben's not going to do anything to me. He's nice. He doesn't want to do anything to hurt me."

"He's a boy; that's enough. Put it on."

I rolled my eyes and slipped the chain over my head. "There. Are you happy now? I look like a total geek."

My mother's most powerful amulet consisted of the dried-up, leathery, nasty-looking leg of a chicken. She got it off a friend of hers who was a voodoo priestess. Mom said it had incredible powers of protection. I was sure it did. Anyone who got a good close look at the gross chicken foot would run away from the person wearing it.

"You just keep that on. And don't forget, I want to see you in front of my tent promptly at ten."

"I know, I know. I'm not a kid anymore, Mom."

"You're not the adult you think you are, either." She scooped up Davide, then paused at the door, coming back into the room to kiss me on the forehead. "Have a nice time. But not too nice."

I gave her a little hug, just enough to show her I

loved her without either of us getting all mushy, patted Davide on his head (which he hates), and turned back to the three drawers that held my clothes.

"I wish I had some girl clothes," I muttered as I went through my things. "Not that this is a date or anything, but still, I wish I had . . ."

A vision popped into my head. Not the kind of vision I get from touching things, but a memory of the first couple of days we were in Germany. We'd just arrived, and Mom had tried to cheer me up by taking me shopping. We each bought soft, lightweight gauze broomstick skirts, Mom's in peach colors, mine in dark blues and purples, along with matching silk peasant shirts. She joked at the time that we could dress up as Gypsies for Halloween. *Those* were girl clothes, and best of all, I didn't look quite so linebacker in them.

Fifteen minutes later, right on the dot of nine, I emerged from the trailer, twitching my skirt to make sure it wasn't tucked up in the waistband, feeling a bit obvious in my girl clothes. There was also the fact that I had a chicken claw under my shirt. . . .

I took three steps before someone loomed up out of the darkness. I shrieked and jumped a foot in the air.

"It's just me," Ben said.

"Well, give me a heart attack, why don't you?" I gasped, clutching at my heart. He moved out of the shadow, into the pool of light cast by one of the nearby lamps. "Oh, I'm so glad you think it's funny. I just bet you won't be laughing when you have to explain my dead body to my mom."

His smile widened. "I haven't seen you in a dress before. You look lovely."

I tugged the neckline of the peasant shirt up, more than a little uncomfortable with the way he was looking at me. It was admiring. Don't get me wrong; I want to be admired, but it just didn't seem right that a guy who looked like him should be giving that look to someone like me. "Yeah, well, I'm a girl. Sometimes I wear girl stuff."

He held out his hand. I hesitated only a few seconds before I took it. We started walking toward the car area. "I'm glad you do, although I hope you won't be too cold riding in a skirt."

I stopped. "Oh. I hadn't thought of that. Maybe I should change—"

He tugged me forward. "No need. I'll make sure you're warm."

I walked a few feet, waiting until we were past a group of people who were laughing as they shoved one another toward the ticket booth. "Um, Ben? You're not still . . . uh . . . hungry, are you?"

He paused, looking down at me. I couldn't see his face, since it was in shadow, but the lamplight shone on his hair, making it black and glossy as ebony. He had it pulled back in a ponytail again, and wore another silk shirt (this one emerald green) and black jeans.

In other words, he was gorgeous as usual. A couple of girls who were giggling at each other stopped to look at him. He ignored them, shifting slightly until I could see he was smiling down at me. "Would it make you feel better to know that I've had dinner?"

I smiled back at him. "Yes, it would."

"Really?" he asked, letting go of my hand to pull his

motorcycle upright. "I will take that as a positive sign."

"Of what?"

He swung a leg over the motorcycle. "Our future. Climb on; we don't have a lot of time if I have to have you back by ten."

I decided to let the "our future" comment go and grabbed his shoulder to steady myself as I got on behind him, tucking my skirt up under my legs so it wouldn't get caught in the wheels.

"No helmets?" I asked.

"Do you want one?"

"Mom would probably have a hissy knowing I went out without one . . ."

He glanced over his shoulder at me, one eyebrow cocked in question.

"It's not against the law, is it?"

"Not here, no. If you were riding with anyone else, I'd say you should wear one, but I will see to it that you come to no harm."

I weighed Mom's potential anger, and decided that just this once, I'd trust Ben. After all, I *was* wearing the horrible protection amulet. "Okay."

"Put your arms around me," he said, still looking over his shoulder at me.

"Uh . . ." I said, hesitating, wondering if I should show him the amulet in case he got any funny ideas.

"It's safer that way. I wouldn't want you to fall off." He looked like he wanted to laugh at me, so I leaned into his back, wrapping my arms around his middle. He started the motorcycle, told me to keep my feet up, and off we went. My head rested against his shoulder, his hair right there under my nose. He smelled good, kind of spicy, not like the aftershave my dad uses that makes me sneeze, but nice. He smelled . . . Ben-ish. I smiled into the back of his neck, my hair whipping back as we bounced off the grass and onto the smooth road, the motor revving as we zoomed into the yawning blackness of the night.

Chapter Seven

"Do you . . . to try . . . back?"

The wind snatched Ben's words away before I could hear them.

"What?" I yelled into his ear.

He waited until he was on a straight stretch of road, then turned his head toward me. "I asked you if you wanted to try driving before we have to go back."

"Really? You'd let me? Sure! I'd love to!"

Ben pulled over to the side of the road, holding the motorcycle steady while I slid off the back. We'd been zooming around the countryside for about a half hour, down long, curvy roads, through a couple of towns, and past a big lake. We were out in the middle of the countryside now, in a rural area where there were no streetlights and only a few houses. Conversation had been limited to Ben asking me a couple of times if I was too cold, and yelling the town names as we approached them. Other than that we just rode through the night, me pressed against the warmth of his back, the rumble of the motorcycle beneath us, and the rush of the wind our buffers against the rest of the world.

Ben slid backward on the seat so I could sit in front of him. He showed me how to use the throttle and clutch on the handlebars, how to brake, where the gearshift was, wrapping it up with a quick lesson in motorcycle physics before allowing me to take charge.

"This is very cool," I said as I settled back against his chest. It was really intimate being pressed up against him like that, with his legs hugging mine, but it was nice intimate, not at all like a guy grabbing your boob or something icky like that. I pursed my lips as I looked down at myself. "Don't look."

"What?"

"Don't look." I had tucked my skirt under my legs, but realized that without Ben blocking the wind, the lightweight material would soon flutter up around me, probably catching in the wheels and killing us both. Or at least me. I rose up, reached between my legs to grab the bottom of the back of my skirt, pulling it forward and tucking it up into my waistband so I was wearing my skirt Gandhi-style. I pushed the stray bits firmly under my legs and sat down. Ben pulled me back against his body (which was really nice, but I had to remind my inner Fran twice that this wasn't a date and she wasn't supposed to go gaga over him), wrapping his arms around my waist in a way that made me feel protected even though he was at my back. I gently let out the clutch, and we were off.

I suppose the best things that can be said about my motorcycle skills are that A) I didn't crash us, and B) I didn't get any bugs in my teeth. I drove along for a while kind of stop-and-start-ish, managed to kill the engine once, and almost tipped us over when I went off the road into the dirt. There was one really fun moment, though. We were on a stretch of road that ran past a winery, a long straight road. The moon was rising, so I could see that there were no cars coming toward us.

"I want to go really fast," I yelled back to Ben. "But we'll go off into the dirt if I do it."

"Lean back," he said, his voice nice and warm against my cold ear.

He let go of my waist and grabbed the handlebars, one arm on either side of me, his foot sliding under mine to the gearshift. The bike bucked beneath us as the engine roared into supersonic mode. All of a sudden we were flying down the road, going so fast I couldn't breathe, almost couldn't see for the wind-whipped tears that snaked from the outer edges of my eyes, the wind molding my shirt to my front like a pair of hands stroking my skin. Our shadows danced blackly along the shoulder of the road, gone in the flick of an eye. It was magical, as if there were nothing in the world but Ben and me and the motorcycle, and an endlessly long black road. I threw my hands into the air and laughed with the sheer joy of going so fast the air was stripped from my lungs.

Ben chuckled in my ear, his lips warm as they nuzzled me, sending a little shimmer of heat down my neck. He slowed down as he came to a sweeping curve at the end of the road, letting me take the controls again. "I've created a monster, I think."

My skin felt all prickly where he had touched me,

but it was a good prickly, a nice prickly. I dragged my mind away from that feeling. No sense in going *there*. "No, but I want a motorcycle now. This is just too fun."

It was also really cold up front despite it being a warm night out, so after about fifteen minutes of my being a biker chick, I agreed to Ben's suggestion that he drive again. We rode back to the Faire without saying anything else, but I couldn't shake the prickly feeling his touch had given me. All of a sudden I wanted to give something back to him for such a wonderful evening.

He parked the bike alongside the far edge of the parking ground, waiting for me to dismount before he turned off the engine. I stood beside the bike, glancing around quickly. We were in the shadows cast by a nearby stand of trees. The people streaming past us didn't even give us a second glance, focused as they were on the bright lights of the Faire.

My stomach twirled around on itself. I wanted to do this, really wanted it, but it was also kind of scary. "Ben?"

"Hmm?" He pocketed his keys and turned to me.

My stomach started turning somersaults. I stepped forward, put my hands on his shoulders, and brushed my lips against his.

He froze, his hands at his sides. I couldn't see his eyes, but I assumed they were black as the sky above. "What was that?"

I let go of his shoulders and stepped back. "It was a kiss."

"It was?" I knew, I just *knew* by the tone of his voice that one of his eyebrows was raised in question.

I also knew that a guy like him—so gorgeous, not to mention at least three hundred years old—had probably kissed a thousand women, all of them better kissers than me. I was certain the French Revolution babe with the legs was. I stepped back another step, feeling positively sick to my stomach now. *Stupid Fran! Stupid, horrible-kisser Fran!*

"Fran?"

I held up my hands and took a step to the side. "It's okay; you don't have to say it. I'm sorry. I won't do it again."

He took my hands, placing them on his chest, his palms warm against the back of my hands as I was pulled gently up against his front. "Now you make me sad. That wasn't a kiss, Fran."

I couldn't look at him. Even if I could see him, I didn't want to look at his eyes. I looked at his earlobe instead, the one with the diamond in it. "I said I'm sorry. You don't have to rub it in that I'm so bad—"

"You're not bad, just inexperienced. Would you like me to kiss you?"

"No," I said, feeling all stubborn and even more stupid than ever. Now he pitied me because I didn't know how to kiss properly. I hate being pitied almost as much as I hate being called a freak.

"All right. How about you kiss me again? This time, don't just brush your lips over mine; keep them there while you say, 'Mississippi.' "

"You're laughing at me."

He let go of my hands on his chest, and slid them around my waist, pulling me closer until his breath feathered across my face as he spoke. "I can assure

91

you that the last thing I want to do now is laugh. Kiss me, Fran. Please."

It was the "please" that did it. I stopped looking at his earlobe, raising my chin a little so my mouth was a hairbreadth from his. "Mississippi," I said, my lips going all warm and soft at the touch of his.

"Again," he whispered.

"Mississippi," I breathed, this time allowing my lips to touch his the whole time I said the word.

"Once more," he said, his voice low and smooth, like black satin.

Mississippi, I thought as I kissed him, really kissed him, my arms sliding up around his shoulders, catching in his hair. I tugged on the leather thong he used to tie back his ponytail, his hair spilling like cool silk over my fingers as his lips moved beneath mine, his mouth opening a little, just enough to suck at my lower lip.

I pulled back from him, slowly, my lips clinging to his like they didn't want to leave (smart lips), my hands trailing over his shoulders and down his chest until they dropped down at my sides, suddenly empty and cold. My brain—what there was of it—ran around like a hamster on a wheel, trying to think of something to say that wasn't, "Holy cow! Do you know how to kiss!"

"Um," I said, then wanted to die. *Um? Come on, Fran; you can do better than that!* "Did you know that your hair is longer than mine?"

He stared at me for a minute, then tipped his head back and shouted with laughter. I turned bright red, I just know I did, because my cheeks went all hot; then suddenly he hugged me, very hard, and let me go.

The hug made me feel better. My hands were on his arms while he hugged me, and I couldn't feel any sense of his mocking me. There was amusement, and pleasure, and a really warm, tingly feeling that I didn't want to look at too closely, but there wasn't any sign he was making fun of me. I relaxed. "I hope you're laughing with me, not at me, 'cause if you're not, you're going to scar me for life and I'll never be able to kiss anyone again without wondering if I totally suck at it."

He took my hand and squeezed it, pulling me toward the Faire. "You don't suck at kissing, Fran. I was laughing because you're such a delight."

A delight. *Hmm. I* thought about that for a couple of minutes as we walked toward my mother's tent, my hand in his, my insides all warm and glowy. Someone thought I was a delight. Made a nice change from freak.

I waved at Mom as she explained a spell to a customer. She looked at her watch, pursing her lips at me. I mouthed, *Sorry!* to her (we were ten minutes late) and pretended I didn't notice her scandalized look when she saw me holding Ben's hand.

"I have to talk to Imogen when she's not busy," I told Ben as we wandered down the center aisle. We stopped to check on Tesla, who was having a snooze, one back leg cocked up on the edge of his other hoof. I patted him, and turned back to Ben. "Thank you for the ride and . . . uh . . . everything."

He smiled at me; then his eyes shifted to Tesla, who

woke up enough to realize that potential treat givers were present, and thus they should be snuffled to see if either had an apple or carrot on their person. We didn't, but I scratched his ears.

"Have you noticed this?" Ben took my hand, using my forefinger to trace an L shape on Tesla's cheek.

"Huh," I said, peering closely at Tesla's coat, my fingers feeling again for the slight thickening. It *was* an L. "What is it?"

"It's a brand."

I wrinkled my nose. "Ew. Why would someone brand him on his face?"

Ben just looked at me for a few seconds, then finally said, "Tesla is a special horse."

"That's what Panna said."

"Panna?"

"The girl whose grandfather owned Tesla. She said that he always told her that Tesla was a special horse."

"He is special. Have you ever heard of a breed called Lipizzan?"

I shook my head. I liked horses, but didn't know too much about them. "Is that why someone put an L on his cheek? Because he's a Lipizzan?"

"Something like that."

"What about the odd-shaped scar on his neck?"

"It's another brand. What did you want to see Imogen about?"

"You're pretty good at changing subjects, aren't you?" I patted Tesla's black nose and started back toward the main fairway. "Are you rich?"

He raised both of his eyebrows. "You're not so bad at subject changing, either. Do you need a loan?"

"No. I just want to know if you've got lots of money. I mean, you mentioned having servants a long time ago. I didn't know if that meant you'd run out, or if you're loaded."

"I think the word is comfortable."

"Oh." I knew what that meant. It was a polite word for rich. "Is Imogen comfortable, too?"

"I would imagine so. Why do you want to know?"

"She shops a lot."

He stopped, putting a hand on my wrist to stop me. "Why the questions, Fran?"

"I just wanted to know if she had oodles of money lying around to shop with, or if she . . ."

"If she what?"

I hesitated. I'd just kissed the guy; I couldn't very well blurt out that I thought his sister might be dipping into Absinthe and Peter's safe to fund her shopping trips. "If she needed some."

"I'm sure if you ask her, she'll tell you."

"Yeah, that's what I thought. I suppose I had better run along. I'm supposed to be learning how to read palms, not that I want to, but Mom says I have to in order to pay for Tesla."

He looked curious. "Do you always do everything your mother says?"

I laughed. "Not even close. But I have to about this, or else I have to find Tesla a new home." I hesitated to tell him more, to explain how confusing it all was— part of me wanting to go home, back to the normal life I had carefully built; but the other part of me, a Fran I didn't know existed, suddenly popped up and said she wanted to keep Tesla, and to stay where Ben was liable to be.

I told that Fran she had things mixed up, and that nothing was worth being a weirdo touchy-feely girl, but she pointed out that I was a weirdo touchy-feely girl no matter where I went, so why shouldn't I have a little fun?

I hate it when I argue with myself. I *never* win.

"I'll see you around, huh? You're going to be here for a little while longer?"

He did the brushing-my-hair-behind-my-ear thing again. "Yes, Imogen has asked me to extend my visit. I'll be here for a bit more."

"Good." A big weight I didn't know was squashing me lifted. I gave him a little smile, deciding that now was as good a time as any to ask him what I wanted to know. "Um . . . can you read minds?"

He didn't even blink at the question; he just answered it. "Not unless I have a bond with the person whose mind I wish to merge with."

"Bond? Oh, you mean . . ." I made slurping noises.

A little teeny-tiny smile curled the edges of his mouth. "Not necessarily. A bond of blood sometimes will be strong enough that I can communicate with the person, but the most powerful connections are between people who have some sort of emotional bond. With trust comes strength."

"Oh, so that's why you can talk to me in my head?"

"You are my Beloved. We are genetically engineered to be able to communicate without words."

"Except when I don't want you to." I thought for a

moment. "If I do the mind-protection thing, could you get through it? I mean, could you force your way into my mind because of this connection we have?"

He didn't say anything. With that silence came a sudden understanding.

"You can't lie to me, can you? That's one of the Dark One rules, isn't it?"

His eyes weren't black, as I expected. The gold bits glittered brightly. "Yes, it's one of the rules."

"So you could force your way into my mind, but you never would because you know it would really cheese me off?"

He looked a bit annoyed. "It goes deeper than that, but that is the basic idea, yes."

"Wow. This is pretty powerful stuff. You'd let me kill you, you can't lie to me . . . is there anything else? I mean, do I have, like, absolute power over you?"

He gave me a really weak smile, kind of like he didn't want to, but couldn't help himself. "There's a lot more, and no, I'm not going to tell it to you. Not until the time comes that you are ready to hear it."

I couldn't help myself. I knew I shouldn't be encouraging this, but I just couldn't help myself. "When will that be?"

"I have no idea." His face was unmoving, the wind ruffling his long hair around his shoulders.

"Oh." I wanted to tell him that I didn't think things were ever going to work out between us, but I didn't. Some part of me, some tiny little part, wanted me to work things out. It kept me silent.

"What are you up to?" he asked. "Whose mind do

you want to read? And what does it have to do with Imogen and money?"

I was a little surprised he didn't know what Mom and Absinthe had cornered me into doing. Soren knew, and although I doubted anyone else did, I was pretty sure either Mom or Absinthe would tell Imogen. For some reason—probably one of those Moravian things—Imogen always seemed to know the latest gossip. But apparently she hadn't told her brother about the thefts.

That was interesting.

It was also icky. I hated feeling suspicious of Imogen. She and Soren were my only friends here.

And Ben. But he wasn't really a friend; he was a Dark One who needed me to bring the light back into his life. . . .

"It's just a little project I'm doing," I finally answered, not wanting to tell him the truth of my suspicions.

"What sort of a project?"

"Nothing you need to worry about. I can handle it, no problem."

I started to walk past him toward Imogen's tent, but he stopped me again. "Fran . . ." His forehead was all wrinkled up in a frown. "If you get into trouble, any trouble, you know I will help you."

"Like with Absinthe? Yeah. I know. And thank you."

"No, not just like the episode with Absinthe. Any trouble—you know that I will help you no matter what the problem. You just have to ask me."

"What makes you think I can't deal with my own

problems?" That warm, glowy feeling inside me fizzled out into annoyance. "You think that just because I'm a girl I need to be bailed out of every situation, right? Well, think again, Benedikt Czerny. This is the twenty-first century. Women don't need guys to do everything for them anymore."

His frown tried to match mine, but I'm the queen of frowns. "I didn't say you couldn't, I simply meant that there are some things that are better left to me. It doesn't lessen your strength to admit that there are some things you can't do."

"Yeah?" I poked him in the chest, just because I knew it would annoy him. How dared he think I couldn't handle my own problems? Patronizing me, that was what he was doing, and I hate being patronized almost as much as I hate to be pitied or thought of as a freak. Patronizing is number three on my list of things I really, really dislike. "You've got that 'I'm so macho, couldn't you just die' look on your face, so you're not fooling me one single bit."

"All I said was that—"

"I know what you said; I'm not stupid! You said if I was too wimpy to deal with my own life, you'd come along like some big, brave vamp knight and rescue my pathetic butt. Ha! I have news for you—my butt doesn't need rescuing. I can do anything you can do. Well . . . with the exception of peeing standing up. And drinking blood. I don't think I could do that; it's just too icky. And the healing thing. And warding stuff, but I could do that if someone taught me how, so that really shouldn't count."

"Fran—"

"Good night, Ben."

Without staying to hear any more of his macho bull, I headed off down the aisle that was growing more and more packed with people every minute. The magic acts were popular, but it was the bands that really brought the crowds out, and as Absinthe had brought with her a German band that had local fans, the crowds were even thicker than normal. I wound my way through them, skimmed around the line of people waiting for Imogen, and presented myself to her, saying, "Peter says you're supposed to show me how to read palms."

She looked a bit surprised at that, glancing at my hands. I turned my back on the people and tugged my gloves out from where I had tucked them into my pocket, pulling them on and taking the chair that Imogen indicated. She was reading a fat man's rune stones, but I figured it wouldn't hurt me to sit and watch how she did her readings.

"How did your ride go?" she asked in between customers.

"Fine. Has your brother always been so pigheaded?"

"Pigheaded?" Her eyebrows rose. "Benedikt?"

Two guys and a girl took the seats across the table from us, arguing about who wanted to go first.

"It doesn't matter." I waved aside my comment.

"Oh, but I think it does," she said, giving me one of her mischievous grins before turning to the threesome and asking who wanted what.

I sat with her for almost two hours, taking a little

break to get some water and to give my mother a chance to run and change for her invocation hour. Imogen showed me all the pertinent points on the palms of those people who came to have her read them, telling me how to interpret the various lumps, lines, bulges, and assorted other hand stuff. It was okay, but to tell the truth, I didn't quite buy it. I guess that was because I knew I could tell a whole lot more about the person just by touching my bare fingers to their palm than by interpreting a big mound of Mars to mean they were particularly argumentative.

I didn't have a chance to talk to her alone until just as the new band was about to start. All of the tents except the piercing one closed down then. Most of the Faire people went in and watched the band, joining in the dancing and stuff. Peter thought it was good for business to have everyone mingling, and said it made for repeat customers. Imogen always went to see the bands, and almost always spent the two hours the band was on dancing with one guy or another, dodging Elvis as he tried to convince her to dance only with him. I usually hung around outside, sometimes talking to Soren, sometimes to Tallulah the medium (she hated music of any sort), sometimes just being by myself.

I waited until Imogen finished with her last customer. She glanced toward the big tent as the loudspeaker crackled into life when Peter announced the band.

"Here, take this," Imogen said, shoving her money box at me. It was crammed full of forints and euros.

"What do you want me to do with it?" I asked, wondering if she had skimmed some off the top for her shopping trips, then immediately felt guilty for even thinking that about someone who was my friend.

"Give it to Peter for me, please. I so want to hear this Picking Scabs."

That was the name of the band, Picking Scabs. I know. It's beyond me, too. I suppose it could be worse. It could be Pickled Scabs.

I gnawed my lip a bit. "Aren't you supposed to count it up and stuff, so you get your fair share?"

"You can do it for me, can't you? Please, Fran?" She stuffed her rune stones in a big leather satchel and gave me a brilliant grin.

"Wait, Imogen, I wanted to ask you . . . uh . . ."

"Yes?" She stood tapping her foot impatiently, her eyes watching all the people streaming into the big tent as the screech of feedback echoed throughout the Faire. The band was evidently about to start.

"Did you go shopping today? I looked for you, but didn't see you."

"Yes, I went into Sopron." That was a big city about ten kilometers down the road. "Was that all you wanted?"

"No. Um. What did you buy?"

She looked at me like my head had turned into a monkey. "Clothes."

"A lot? I mean, did you find a lot of good bargains?"

She laughed her tinkly little laugh that reminded me of a stream burbling. "Fran, I never buy bargains. Those are for the peasants."

She traced a quick ward above my head, and dashed off toward the big tent. I sighed. So much for my detective skills. I'd been questioning people all day and was no farther than when I started. Except now I knew that possibly everyone connected to the Faire could have had a shot at the safe . . . but I had felt only seven people on the safe's handle. It didn't make sense. It just didn't make sense.

I spent ten minutes counting Imogen's take, writing up the info on her slip and tucking it neatly into the box. Then I went to hunt down Peter.

"Hey, Peter. Imogen gave me this to give to you. I counted the money and wrote it on the slip."

"What?"

Peter was at the back of the tent with Teodor the security guy/bouncer who kept an eye on everyone. Peter's little balding head was bopping along with the music, which was loud, loud, and then more loud. The bass positively throbbed in my teeth it was so loud. The lead singer screamed in German into the microphone. I always crank my headphones up when I'm listening to music—loud is definitely better than soft—but this was ridiculous! The sound screeching from the big amps was so pervasive it filled everything, every space, both inside the tent and inside the people. I felt it crawling around the edges of my brain and knew then that Absinthe had managed to find a band that knew some sort of magic. Probably they cast a spell to make the audience adore them—Imogen said that was pretty standard stuff.

I repeated my words, bellowing them about four inches from his ear. It was barely enough to be heard.

He nodded and took the cash box, tucking it under his arm to applaud as the music stopped.

I didn't want to touch him. I had touched more people in the last day than I had in a month, and I wanted my brain back to myself. I spent a few seconds being mad that my mother had manipulated me into the position of having to do the thing I hated most, but then my inner Fran pointed out that I had offered to do it in exchange for something I wanted.

I hate it when my brain does that sort of thing.

The next song started. I decided there was no way I could possibly come right out and ask Peter if he was stealing from himself for some purpose I couldn't begin to imagine, gritted my teeth, and peeled off the glove from my left hand, edging my way closer to him. He was bouncing and bopping around in that "I'm cool and I can dance" way that adults think make them look like they know how to dance (which they don't). I let my hand brush against him a couple of times, turning so it was my palm that touched his arm. He never even noticed when I backed away.

I noticed, though. I backed into Ben.

"Hi," I yelled, trying to be nonchalant, like I didn't care whether he was there or not, but failing when he grinned at me. I couldn't resist his grins. They made me go all warm and puddly inside.

"Dance?" he yelled back, and tipped his head toward the mass of people dancing like crazy in the main area of the tent.

"Sure."

He grabbed my hand, looked down, and, without even asking me, peeled off my gloves and stuffed them in his back pocket. He held out his hand for the other gloves. I gave them to him. He pushed us through the crowd until we were in the middle of the pack. There must have been three hundred people jammed into that tent, all dancing like mad. Ben kept a hand on me as we joined in, but it was hard going, since every two seconds someone's elbow bumped me, or leg jostled me, or arm hit my back, or hair swung out.

"This is like dancing in a can of sardines," I yelled in Ben's ear.

"Do you want to leave?" he yelled in mine.

"Not now. Maybe in a bit."

I swear, someone in the band was using magic, because everything started to get better. Ben smiled, and somehow managed to keep us moving so hardly anyone smacked into us. I kept my hands on his arms, and gave myself up to the moment. The music didn't seem nearly so harsh and annoying, and started to make sense. Along the fringes of the dance area I could see Mom dancing with a laughing Peter. Imogen had evidently given Elvis the go-ahead, because they were dancing near us, Imogen looking a little bored, Elvis all but drooling on her. Even Soren was dancing, with a girl, yet! I smiled at him and swung around when Ben turned us, just barely avoiding Kurt's long hair as he did a little twirl with a tall blond woman.

"Everyone's here," I yelled happily to Ben, feeling for once like I was truly a part of a group, nothing special, just me, just one little cog in a great big wheel.

"They have to be; the lead singer's using a glamour," he answered. "It makes people want to dance. Can't you feel it?"

"Yeah, but I don't mind. Hey, look, there's Absinthe." He looked where I pointed. I've never seen Absinthe even near the tent when the bands played, but there she was, her spiky pink hair bobbing up and down as she danced with Karl.

"I'm so happy," I said, and threw my hands up as Ben laughed with me, grabbing my waist to spin me around. "Everything's so wonderful!"

I realized my mistake the second my fingers came in contact with the bodies surrounding me. Images, thoughts, hopes, desires, sadness, sickness, sorrow . . . As Ben spun me around, a hundred thoughts filled my mind. I pulled my arms back in, but not before I touched someone.

Someone bad.

Someone evil.

Someone who was planning on killing the laughing, handsome man who held me in his arms.

Chapter Eight

"Are you all right?"

"Yeah. You can let go of my head now."

I sat up slowly, as if I had been feeling dizzy and was liable to pass out at any moment. I wasn't the least bit dizzy, but I was *very* sick to my stomach.

Someone wants to kill Ben!

Ben squatted next to the chair he'd led me to when I pretended to collapse inside the tent. I took a few deep breaths of fresh air, air not polluted by hundreds of bodies, and looked around me. We were outside Tallulah's tent, which was the farthest point away from the main tent. The music was a dull throb in the back of my head, like a headache that wouldn't go away. I didn't remember walking all the way here, and wondered if Ben had carried me. Wouldn't I remember that?

Someone wants to kill Ben!

I shook my head and closed my eyes again. Thinking was too hard to do with the music pounding away in my brain.

"Is she better? Does she want water?"

Someone wants to kill Ben!

"Shut up," I growled to the shrieking inner Fran.

"Did she just tell me to shut up?"

"I'm not sure. It sounded like it."

A shadow fell between us, on top of my hands, which were clutching Ben's as if I had been drowning. It must be Tallulah. She hated the bands; she always stayed away from the tent when one was playing.

"Someone wants to kill you." I didn't think I had said the words, but I did. It was my voice, and Ben's fingers tightened around mine.

"Someone always wants to kill me," Tallulah said very matter-of-factly. "That's no reason to tell me to shut up. It's because I can contact those who have passed on, and tell things the living don't always want made public. Once, a lady in Amsterdam who had suffocated her elderly father tried to kill me with a hatpin. A hatpin! Naturally, I knew she was coming. Sir Edward told me." Sir Edward is Tallulah's boyfriend. He's dead, but they still hang out together.

"I don't think that Fran is talking about you," Ben said, not looking in the least bit surprised or worried or freaked or any of the ways I would feel if I were told that someone wanted me deader than a squashed bug. He was just looking at me, a little concerned, true, but his eyes were back to honey oak with gold flecks.

I glanced up at Tallulah and gave her a feeble smile. "I wasn't telling you to shut up, and I'm glad you have Sir Edward so you'll know whenever someone wants to off you, but Ben's right. This is about him, not you."

"Someone wants to kill Ben?" Tallulah stepped

back and stared at him. Mom says Tallulah is related to a gypsy queen, and I have to admit, she looks like it. Her skin is the color of a double-tall latte, but her eyes are bright, bright blue. She has long black hair with a big white streak on one side, and she always wears her hair in a big blobby bun on the back of her neck. She's older than Mom, but it's hard to tell just how old she is, because there's not a single wrinkle on her face, and even Mom has a couple of lines around her eyes. "Why would anyone wish to kill Ben?"

They both looked at me. "Don't stare at me like that; I don't know why. I don't even know who it was; there were too many people pushed up around us, all I felt was someone wanted Ben sta . . . um . . . dead."

I know what you're thinking. There I was a few hours after telling Ben I could handle my own problems without his assistance, thank you very much, and what did I do? I spilled everything. The thing is, I'm not stupid. I know I can handle my own stuff—dealing with Mom's demands, pinning down the likeliest person to have taken the money—but this was different. This was Ben's life at stake. (Ow! Pun not intended.) He needed to hear it so he could get the heck out of Dodge before the staker got to him.

My hands shook in his. I knew he felt them shaking, but he didn't say anything. He just gave my fingers a little squeeze, then let go of my hands and stood up, pulling my gloves out of his back pockets. I put them on, mentally swearing an oath that I was never going to take them off again.

Yeah, okay, I knew it was an oath I wasn't going to keep, but it felt good there for about ten seconds.

"Can you walk, or do you want me to carry you again?"

Rats! He *had* carried me to Tallulah's and I had been too weirded out to notice it. "I can walk. I'm okay, just a little freaked. Thanks for letting me sit here, Tallulah."

"You know you're always welcome, Fran." She gave Ben a long look as I got to my feet. "I believe I shall contact Sir Edward and ask him what he knows about this."

Ben made a graceful bow to her. She inclined her head, and for a moment I could see why people thought she was related to royalty. I waggled my fingers at her and started off toward our trailer, Ben at my side. He didn't try to hold my hand, which was okay, except I kind of wanted him to.

"You want to tell me what happened? What really happened, not the Tallulah version. Everything, from the time you walked into the tent to when you felt sick."

I chewed my lip, deciding on a little judicious editing. "I didn't feel anything other than the glamour, and I didn't even feel that at first. To tell you the truth, I thought the music was kind of bad."

A smile flickered across his face. "It *was* bad. Hence the need for the glamour."

A glamour, for those of you not hip to the latest magic lingo, is a form of magic used to change the perception about something, usually from bad to good—in other words, someone in the band was using a glamour to make everyone think they were wonderful, giving them the overpowering desire to dance to their music. Lots of people can do glamours—witches, demon lords, vamps . . . it really is pretty common stuff. I'd just never experienced it before, since I'd always stayed away from Mom's weirdo friends.

"Then you asked me to dance, and everything started to be fun." I slid a glance at him to see if he thought I was enjoying myself because I was dancing with him as opposed to the glamour starting to affect me, but we were walking behind Elvis's trailer, and Ben was in the shadow. "And then the next thing I knew, I was being swamped by people's minds. Then I touched him."

Ben stopped. "Him? It was a man?"

I stopped, too, chewing my lip as I tried to remember (okay, so chewing my lip is a little nervous habit I have; I never said I was perfect). I closed my eyes and sorted through the emotions I remembered feeling. With the exception of the girl who was worried because she thought she was pregnant, it was impossible to tag the fleeting images by the person's gender. "I'm sorry; I can't tell. It was over so quickly, just a flash in my mind of someone who was filled with thoughts of staking you. Someone cold and black and"—I shivered and rubbed my arms—"extremely evil inside. Whoever it is, Ben, they mean business. You need to be careful, because this person really wants you dead."

"Hmm."

He started walking again. I followed, rolling my eyes. He was back to his tough-guy macho routine.

"You know, I read a lot of mysteries," I said.

"Do you?"

"Yeah, so I know all about someone wanting someone else dead, and detectives in the books always say that the who isn't important; it's the why. If you know why someone wants you dead, it'll tell you who it is. So who wants to see you staked?"

He waited for me to catch up to him, then walked beside me with absolutely no expression on his face. "Quite a few people, I imagine."

I goggled at him (something I'm not proud of, but hey, it had been a stressful day). "You're joking. Why would someone want you dead? You haven't, like, accidentally killed someone when you were having dinner, have you?" I couldn't imagine Ben doing something bad enough to make someone want to kill him. I'd been inside his mind; I knew what sort of person he was—tormented, in a lot of pain, yes, but he wasn't bad. He didn't like to hurt people.

"I'm a Moravian Dark One. Many people think we're the evil creatures of vampire legend, preying on the innocent, changing people to our own kind, damning them to eternal hell. Most vampire hunters don't bother to find out what we are; they lump us in with demons, ghouls, and the like. Such people kill us simply because we *are*, Fran. They don't need any other reason."

"But that's wrong! You're not evil; you're just a little different from anyone else. For that matter, I'm different, but I don't see anyone trying to knock me off."

He didn't say anything to that. I was starting to figure him out—what he didn't say was often as important as what he did. "You know, this thing where you can't lie to me makes me nervous. Does your not saying anything mean that you think someone is trying to kill me?"

He put his hand on my shoulder. I had to point out to my inner Fran that it was just a nice, comforting gesture, not a romantic one. "No, I don't. But your mother is a witch; you must know the history of witches through the ages."

"Yeah, I know about witch hunts and all that, but people don't do that anymore."

His silence filled the air between us.

"They do?"

"In some places, yes. But you have nothing to worry about. Your mother protects you, as does your own desire to blend in, and . . ."

"And what?"

He didn't say anything, but he pulled his arm off my shoulder. I had an idea of what he was going to say, and I didn't want to hear it. I didn't even want to think it, because then I'd get mad at him and his macho attitude.

So I didn't say anything either, and we both walked along in silence until Ben broke it. "Will you be all right alone until your mother comes back?"

"Sure, I stay by myself all the time." And usually I enjoyed being left alone, but tonight I wanted Ben to stay. I tried to think up a reason to keep him with me. "Are you hungry? Would you like a cup of tea? We have— Oh." I am *so stupid! Duh, Fran, he's a vampire;*

you were just talking about that. "I'm sorry; sometimes I forget that you're a . . . Sometimes I forget."

I hurried forward, trying to pretend I didn't have a mouth as big as Colorado.

"Thank you, Fran."

"For what?" I asked miserably. "Putting my foot in my mouth . . . *again?*"

"For not letting it matter to you what I am."

I shrugged, but allowed the warm glow of his words to beat back some of the freaked-out feeling inside me. "I've never understood why people blame someone for what they were born being. It's not like they have any choice, is it? I mean, I don't have a choice about being a psychometrist any more than you have a choice about being a Dark One. We just are. So why get bent out of shape over something we can't change? My mom always says it's not who you are, but what you do that matters."

"Such words of wisdom from a girl who thinks of herself as a freak."

I glanced at him to make sure he wasn't laughing at me. He wasn't. "Yeah, well, it's not so much that I think I'm a freak, but other people do, and, you know, it gets old really fast being different from everyone else."

"Tell me about it," he said, stopping in front of our trailer. "You've lived with being different for only four years; I've lived with it for three hundred and twelve."

"Wow, you really are old," I said, awed by the thought of living so long.

He smiled, then leaned forward and gave me a little

tiny kiss, probably an Iowa's worth of a kiss. "Yeah, I'm old, but not so old that I don't know a good thing when I see it. Go on in. I'll catch up with you tomorrow night."

It took me a couple of seconds to shut the inner Fran up (she was squealing over the kiss). "Where are you going? Back to the main tent? You're not going to go back there with the psycho who wants to stake you, are you?"

"I'm not afraid, Fran."

I stared at him, my eyes all big and googly. "Well, you should be! Ben, I'm not joking when I say the person who wants you dead is bad, really bad, Grade-A evil, in fact. You don't want to mess with him or her, whoever it is. Trust me, this person's thoughts were lovingly dwelling on the joy of watching you die a horrible, painful death."

He tucked a strand of my hair behind my ears. "Go inside, Fran. I'll be all right."

"Argh!" I yelled, wanting to strangle him and shake him and kiss him all at once. "You are the most frustrating guy in the whole wide world! Fine! Go back and get yourself killed. See if I care!"

I stomped up the stairs, slamming the door to the trailer behind me. Davide looked up as I threw my bag onto the chair and stormed down the narrow aisle. "Stupid Ben. Stupid, stupid, stupid Ben. Oh, he's so friggin' tough, no one can kill him. Ha! Well, who needs him? I sure don't. If he wants to get himself killed, that's just peachy keen with me. Just means I don't ever have to redeem his soul, however you do *that.* He doesn't matter to me, not one little bit. Him and his long hair and his nummy body and the motorcycle and that wonderful way he kisses—none of it matters! Not one stupid iota!"

Davide made a face that looked remarkably like he was pursing his lips at me.

"And you can just stop looking at me like that! It's not my problem!"

I swear he raised his eyebrows at me.

I pointed my finger at him. "Not one word from you, cat. I tried to warn him. I told him flat-out that he was stupid to tangle with whoever it is who wants him dead, but he's all 'I'm a Dark One. I can do anything' to me. Dark One—*Dork One* is more like it."

Okay, so that was unfair—there was nothing dorky about Ben—but I wasn't about to admit that to a cat.

Davide stood up, arched his back in a stretch, then sat down and curled his tail around his feet while he gave me a yellow-eyed look that spoke louder than words.

"I did everything I could!" I said, yanking the closet open to get my pillow and blanket. "There's nothing else I can do!"

He just kept staring at me. I peeled off my gloves and threw them on the floor. "*Gah!* All right! Stop it! I'll go save Ben's butt. Are you happy? Everyone will probably find out about me because of this, and then someone will do a witch hunt on me, and I'll end up dead, and *then* who'll give you the good tuna, huh? It's on your head now, buster!"

I snatched up my keys and stomped out of the trailer, muttering to myself as I headed toward the loud pulse of music. This far out, the glamour was too diluted to work, and my original opinion about the band was justified. They really did suck.

The area outside of the tent was absolutely devoid of people, which was unusual even when a band was playing. Usually people wandered out to use the portable toilets, or to have a smoke, but not tonight. There wasn't a single person to be seen all the way down the main aisle, all the smaller tents were black and closed up. Even Tallulah's was shut down. A few chip wrappers and empty cups were kicked along the ground by the slight breeze, but other than that, nothing moved.

It was really very eerie.

I slipped into the back of the main tent, pressing against the canvas wall, trying to keep myself out of the way of the people, and as far away from the power of the glamour as was possible. What I really needed was a way to—

"Imogen!"

A few feet away Imogen stood swaying to the music, Elvis and another guy arguing violently next to her. That was a common enough sight—Elvis got really jealous when Imogen danced with other guys. Usually she ignored him. "Imogen!"

She turned and smiled at me. I motioned her over. "You're just the person I want to see."

"Isn't that sweet of you, Fran! Why aren't you dancing?"

I waved her question away. Already I could feel the glamour working, making me want to drop everything and join in the happy dancing throng. "No time for that. Is there a ward that can protect you from a glamour?"

She smiled at the guy who was now threatening the much smaller Elvis with two big fists. "I hope he knocks him out; Elvis has been so persistent tonight. Yes, of course there is a ward; there is a protection ward for everything."

"Can you show me how to do it? If it's not a Moravian secret, that is. Something I could use specifically against this glamour?" My toes started tapping against my will. My legs wanted me to plunge into the crowd.

She turned to me with a slight frown between her brows. "Why would you want to be protected against this glamour? It's not a harmful one, and the band sounds much better with it."

"Please, Imogen, I don't have time to explain. Could you just show me the ward?"

She gave me a curious look, then turned so her body was blocking the view of anyone who might glance our way. I had a hard time paying attention to her instructions; the music was so persuasive that everything in me cried out to go dance, to have fun, to let it fill me and wipe away all my worries.

She drew the ward on me, then showed me how to draw it. The thing with wards is not actually in drawing the symbol correctly; it's the belief you put behind it. That's the way it is with all magic—believe, and it works. Doubt, and the power of the magic weakens. I had no doubt of my own abilities—such as they were—which helped me draw the ward. The second my finger traced the last curve, the symbol glowed into life in the air in front of me, a bright gold shimmering that immediately dissolved. The feeling of protection remained, however.

I had done it! I had drawn a ward, and it worked! "Ugh!" I yelled, and clapped my hands over my ears. "Man, they are *so* bad!"

Imogen laughed and turned back to the music, holding out her hands for the guy who stood over the crumpled form of Elvis. Evidently the guy had heard Imogen's wish, because he rubbed his knuckles before taking Imogen's hands and dancing off with her. I went over and prodded Elvis with my toes, but he didn't move. His chest rose and fell, though, so I knew he wasn't dead, just knocked out. "Sorry, I have more important things to do," I told him as I turned toward the dancing crowd, skirting along the edges as I looked for Ben. For a moment my ward flared to life, an ugly black, but just as quickly the image of it dissolved. I figured whoever was making the glamour had added a little power to it, but as long as my ward held, it didn't concern me.

I hesitated as I watched everyone dancing, hating what I had to do, my mind squirreling frantically for another option, but there was none. Ben thought he could take on the person who wanted him dead, but I knew the truth. Whoever it was, man or woman, was cold with desperation, wholly committed body and soul to seeing Ben dead. You don't get that sort of determination in your average vampire hunter. At least, I didn't think you did.

"No pain, no gain," I told myself and, taking a deep breath, plunged into the crowd. I let my hands touch everyone, not trying to guide them, just allowing myself to be jostled around randomly. People, images, objects, emotions, moments in time, thoughts, wishes, fears—everything that people carry around in their subconscious filled my brain until I thought my head was going to burst, pain lancing through my entire body with the effort to hold it all. I couldn't breathe; there were so many people pressing in on me, filling me, so many of them they pushed me aside and took over. There was nothing left of me, not one little bit left; it was all them. Just as I was sure my mind was fracturing, at the exact moment when I knew I was stepping over the line of sanity to insanity, blackness filled me, a soft, warm, velvet blackness. It shut out the voices, the images, the people who filled me. The blackness covered me, protecting me in a soft cocoon, slowly separating me from the crowd until I slipped into a long, dark, inky pool that seemed to welcome me with a warm embrace and a whisper that all would be well.

Chapter Nine

"Hey," Soren said.

"Hey. Oooh, almond croissants?"

He nodded and plopped down beside me, waiting patiently for me to return the paper bag I'd snatched out of his hands. There were two things I really liked about being in Europe—castles (very cool), and the way everybody went to the local bakery every morning to get fresh-baked stuff. The bread was good, but the almond croissants . . .

"Mmm," I said blissfully, allowing the featherlight flakes of croissant to melt on my tongue. "It's probably got a gazillion calories, but man, this is good."

Soren tore off one of the two curved arms of a croissant and popped it in his mouth, chewing as he squinted into the morning sun. Bruno and Tesla grazed in front of us, throwing elongated, wavering shadows as they moved slowly across the edge of the meadow, chomping happily at the grass, their tails keeping a lazy rhythm as they switched at flies. I love this time of the morning. It isn't late enough to be really hot, but it's warm enough to make your spirits soar. A couple of blue-green dragonflies skimmed low over the grass, then headed off toward the trees, where a thin stream trickled.

"How do you feel?" Soren finally asked.

I finished my croissant before answering, wrapping my arms around my legs and propping my chin on my knees as I sucked the last sweet, almondy bits of croissant from my teeth. "I'm fine; why do you ask?"

"Why do I ask? You had some sort of panic attack last night and had to be carried out of the main tent. You don't normally do that. I thought you might be sick or something."

"Carried?" I rested my cheek on my knee and looked at Soren. His nose was peeling from a sunburn he'd gotten a few days ago. "Who carried me?"

He picked at the grass, throwing a handful at the horses. "Benedikt."

Drat with bullfrogs on it. Twice Ben had carried me, and both times I'd been too out of it to notice. I looked back at the horses. "Dr. Bitner said I could ride Tesla if I wanted, as long as I didn't take him out on the road, 'cause he doesn't have any shoes, and I shouldn't push him too far. He said I should start slow, and build his stamina up, but that he was so old he'd never really be able to be ridden a lot."

Soren slid me a sidelong glance. "Why are you changing the subject?"

"That's what people do when they don't want to talk about something."

He thought about that for a minute, then asked (just like I knew he would), "Why don't you want to talk about what happened last night?"

I picked a buttercup and held it under his chin. He batted it away. "If I tell you what happened last night, will you show me how to ride?"

He looked at Tesla. "Bareback?"

"I don't have a saddle."

"You don't have a bridle, either."

I shrugged. "Can't I use the nylon lead rope and his halter?"

He shrugged, too. "It won't have a . . . what do you call it . . ." He made a gesture across his mouth.

"Bit?"

"Yes, bit. But I will show you if you tell me what happened."

"If I tell you, you have to swear not to tell anyone. Not your father, or anyone. Got that?"

His eyes widened. "Is it something to do with the theft?"

"No. Yes. No, not really. It's something to do with me. Do you swear?"

"Ich schwöre." He spat on his hand and held it out for me to shake. *Ew.* I grabbed the very tips of his fingers and shook them. "What happened?"

"You won't believe me if I just tell you. What do you have in your pockets?"

He looked surprised, a little puzzled frown pulling his eyebrows together, but he stuck a hand into his shorts pocket and pulled out the contents. There was a small blue plastic comb, a few coins, string, a used bandage, a set of keys, and a tube of lip balm. I peeled my gloves off and plucked the keys from his hand.

"You've never shown me these keys before, have you?"

He shook his head.

"Right." I separated one key from the rest and held it up, allowing the images the key conveyed to tell me about its use. "This key is to the big wooden chest your dad keeps his props in. The big props."

Soren's eyes widened as he looked at the key; then he nodded. I picked out a second key. "Trailer." His eyes widened even further. I held up a tiny little key. "This is to a violin case. I didn't know you played the violin."

He jaw dropped. "No one knows except Papa and *Tante.* How do you do that?"

I help up another key. "This one unlocks the big box you keep the doves in. What's it called—a dovecote? Whatever, this key is new. You haven't had it long."

I thought his eyes were going to pop out of his head, so I wrapped up my show, setting the keys gently into his hand. "It's nothing special, Soren. I can feel things by touching them, that's all."

"That's all? It is too special; it's very special!" He looked down at my hands like they were painted purple or something. I pulled my gloves back on. The sun was still shining, but all of a sudden I felt like a cloud had passed overhead. "I can't believe you can do that. Is that why you wear gloves? Can you do it with people, too? Can you read my mind if you touch me? Can you tell everything I'm thinking?"

I got up and walked over to Tesla, who paid absolutely no attention to me, having checked me over for apples earlier (I had carrots, which he graciously accepted). Tesla and Ben seemed to be the only ones who didn't care about my curse. How sad is that? "If I touched you with my bare hand, yes, I could tell what you're thinking. Kind of. More like what strong emotions you're feeling at the time."

Soren sucked in his breath, looking at me as if I were dancing naked. Upside down. I threw my arms out, annoyed that he of all people should make a big deal about a little difference. "I'm still the same person I was a few minutes ago, Soren! You didn't think I was weird then!"

"I didn't say I think you are weird," he said slowly.

"You don't have to say it; that look says it all. I've seen it before, you know. Everyone who finds out about this has that same look, the 'Fran is a freak' look. I thought you would understand what it was like to be born with something you can't do anything about. It's nothing different from you being born with one leg shorter than the other."

His face turned red as he looked down at his leg. "My leg can't tell me what you're thinking."

"And my hands can, yeah, so? I can't turn it off, Soren. I just have to live with it. I thought you'd understand. Now I'm sorry I told you."

I turned away from him, leaning on Tesla's side, tracing my fingers over the scar on his shoulder, blinking furiously so Soren wouldn't see me cry.

"Fran?"

I twisted the ends of Tesla's mane into a braid, sick that I'd ruined my friendship with Soren. "What?"

"I don't think you're weird. I think . . . I think it's cool."

"It's not cool; it's a curse," I mumbled down at my hands. Tesla's white mane was tangled between my fingers. That was what my life had turned into, a tangle. I was tangled up with Mom and the Faire, tangled up with Ben, tangled with Soren and Imogen, tangled with Tesla. . . .

"I don't think so." Soren came around to the other side of Tesla. "I really do think it's neat. I'm sorry if I made you feel bad."

I twitched a shoulder. "I'm used to it."

He looked down at my hands. "Can you do it with animals?"

"Tell what they're feeling? No. I think it's because they think differently. The only things I pick up on are human emotions and stuff like that."

"Oh." He looked thoughtful for a few minutes. "Still, I bet that could be useful."

"Useful!" I snorted. "Yeah, if you want everyone to jump back every time you come near them because they're afraid to let you touch them, then it's useful. Otherwise it's a curse, like I said."

"That's why Miranda wanted you to find out who's stealing our money, isn't it? She wants you to touch everyone and see who is the thief?"

I combed through Tesla's mane with my fingers. "Something like that, yeah."

His eyes widened again. "You touched me the other

day, I remember! You touched me with your bare hand. Were you reading me then?"

I chewed on my lip and tried to think of a polite way to tell him that there was a short time when I thought he might be a suspect. "Well . . . I had to eliminate everyone who touched the safe—"

"Was I a suspect? You thought I was a suspect? Cool!"

I rolled my eyes, bending to check that Tesla's hobble was on correctly. The leather cuffs around his front feet weren't tight, and the chain that connected them was long enough to let him graze without giving him the full range of his normal stride. "You are the only person I know who thinks it's cool to be a suspect."

"I've never been a suspect before," he explained, limping after me as I walked back toward the Faire. "I wish you had told me. I would have liked to write it in my journal."

"You can write it in there now."

"Am I still a suspect?"

I stopped and waited for him to catch up to me. "No, of course not. You checked out."

"I checked out," he said in an awe-filled voice. "That's cool, too."

"Whatever."

We walked down the long length of the Faire, swallows wheeling and diving ahead of us as they did their aerobatic act between the tents. "What happened after Ben carried you home?"

"I don't know."

He pursed his lips. "You don't know?"

"Nope. I was out. I don't remember anything except waking up this morning."

"What did Miranda say?"

"Zzzzzz."

"What?" Soren stopped to gawk at me.

I smiled. "She was asleep when I got up this morning. I assume that Ben hauled me back to the trailer, and Mom tucked me in. That's all."

"Oh." He looked a bit disappointed by that and evidently decided to go after something more promising. "Who is a suspect? Who do you think stole the money?"

I stopped at the fringe between the Faire and the trailers. It was still too early for most of the people to be up, but a few bleary-eyed people staggered out of their cars with cups of coffee and bags of baked goods clutched in their hands, heading for their trailers. "I don't know. Seven people touched the safe, and of those seven, almost all of them check out."

"Almost all?"

"I haven't talked to the last couple of people."

"Oh." He sucked the inside of his cheek for a moment as we watched Absinthe, a lurid pink scarf that clashed with her hair tied around her head, and a pair of black glasses hiding her eyes, slip out the door of Kurt and Karl's trailer. She went straight for her trailer.

"That was interesting," I said.

He made a face. "Not really. So, last night, when you had your attack—"

"It wasn't an attack," I interrupted. I mean, sheesh, I felt weird enough; I didn't need people thinking I had attacks, too!

"Okay, when whatever happened to you happened, that was because . . ." His nose scrunched up. "Why *did* it happen?"

I kicked at a rock, prying it out of the sod so I could toss it into the garbage can nearby. "I think it was overload. I've never touched more than a couple of people a day, and in there, I was touching hundreds. I felt like I was being crushed by them, like I was just an empty shell. It was awful."

"Ben touched you."

"Yeah."

Soren turned blue eyes full of accusation on me. "He knows, doesn't he? You told him, but you didn't tell me."

I tried for a supportive smile. I don't think I succeeded. "I told you now; that's gotta count for something."

"You didn't trust me, and you trusted him. You only just met him!"

"Come on," I said, tugging him toward the trailer Absinthe had just left.

"You like him more than me, don't you?"

"Oh, for Pete's sake . . ." I stopped and shook him. "This isn't a contest, okay? Ben knows because . . . because . . . because he just knows! I didn't tell him; he figured it out himself."

"You didn't tell him?" Soren's eyes were narrowed; he was suspicious despite obviously wanting to believe me.

"I didn't tell him; he guessed. Feel better? Good. Now come on; I need some help."

"Help with what?"

"I need to touch Karl."

Soren's eyes bugged out again. I smacked him on the arm.

"Not that kind of touch, stupid! I need to *touch* him. He's one of the people who used the safe. I need to see if he feels cold and desperate inside."

Cold. Desperate. Just like the person who wanted Ben dead. I sucked in my breath and thought about that for a moment. Could it be? Could the thief be the same person who wanted Ben staked? Why?

"Fran? You okay? You're not going to have another attack, are you?"

I made mean eyes at him. "I do not have attacks!"

"Okay, but you're scaring me. Your eyes went all funny. What's the matter?"

"Nothing. I just need to think for a minute." I looked around, then grabbed Soren's hand, dragging him over to a couple of plastic crates that were stacked behind Elvis's trailer, out of sight of the rest of the trailers. "Sit."

He sat. He also watched me as I paced back and forth, trying to figure it all out. "I'm going to do this the way the detectives do it in books."

Soren dug a small, grubby notebook out of his pocket. "I'll be your trusted sidekick."

I stopped pacing to give him a look.

"What? That's not right?"

"We're not in a Western, Soren. This is serious."

"You're the boss." He looked thrilled. I felt peeved.

"Point one," I said, resuming pacing and ticking each item off on my finger. "Someone stole the Faire money, not once but three times in the last ten days."

"Yes." Soren bent over his notebook, his tongue peeking out as he wrote with a broken pencil.

"Point two: Seven people touched the safe—your father and aunt, you, Imogen, my mother, Elvis, and Karl."

"Hey!" Soren looked up. "Elvis! I bet it's him."

"You're jumping ahead. Trusty sidekicks never jump ahead."

His lips made an O. "Sorry."

"Point three: It doesn't make sense for either Absinthe or Peter to steal from themselves and make a big stink about it."

"Big stink," Soren repeated as he wrote.

"Point four: Elvis is a demonologist. Demons can get into anything if they are so ordered."

"Yeah," Soren said, his eyes lighting up.

"Except something made of steel," I added. His face fell.

"Oh. The safe is made of steel."

"Exactly. So unfortunately, although I'd like the suspect to be Elvis, I just don't see how he could use a demon to switch the money with the bits of newspaper that your aunt found."

He sighed noisily. "I can't either."

"Point five: Your dad left the combination to the safe lying around where anyone could see it, but only seven people touched the safe, so that eliminates everyone else."

Soren looked thoughtful, sucking on the end of the broken pencil. "That leaves Imogen, Miranda, and Karl."

"Exactly. And since Ben says Imogen doesn't need money, and I know my mom wouldn't steal anything, that leaves—"

"Karl!"

"Someone my name in vain is taking?"

Soren jumped up and I whirled around to see Karl dressed in a tank top, jogging shorts, and tennis shoes. Karl didn't speak English as well as the rest of the Faire people, but to give him credit, he spoke it better than I spoke German.

"Oh, hi, Karl. Uh . . ." I slipped my gloves off of my hand as I held it behind my back. Soren, who stood behind me, suddenly rushed forward.

"Karl, I was trying to show Fran the trick you do with the coin—you know, the one where you make it come out of someone's nose? I can't do it as well as you. Would you show it to her?"

I blinked for a second, then nodded my head. "Yes, would you please? I'd love to learn some magic."

Karl didn't look like he believed either of us, but he obligingly pulled a coin out of Soren's ear, my eyebrow, and his own elbow.

"Wow, that's really cool; can I try it?" I asked, holding out my bare hand.

Karl gave me the coin, his fingers brushing my hand as he dropped it onto my palm. "It's not a difficult trick, but much practice it takes."

I made a couple of fumbled passes with the coin, then gave up with a laugh, handing it back to him. "Guess I'm not cut out to be a magician. Thanks anyway. Happy jogging." I let my fingers touch his hand for a second longer than was necessary, then waved as he trotted off toward the road.

"Well?" Soren asked as soon as Karl was out of hearing.

I sat down on the crate. "We can cross him off. He didn't feel at all guilty."

Soren looked up as his father called for him. "I have to go."

I waved him off. "That's okay, I've got some stuff to do for my mom. I'll see you later."

"Yes, later. I am to show you how to ride, don't forget." He stuffed the notebook in his pocket. "And we'll work on this, too. We will come up with other points; don't worry."

I let him run off without telling him that I wasn't worried in the least. I already knew of one more.

Point six: Someone who was on the dance floor last night would have given his or her soul to see Ben dead, and my gut instinct told me that that person and the thief were one and the same . . . and there were only two names left on my list of suspects.

Imogen and my mother.

Chapter Ten

This was our last day outside of Kapuvár. The next morning we'd pack everything up, and head off for Budapest, where we'd stay for ten days. Although my mom and I had only been with the Faire for a month, I'd decided I liked playing the smaller towns better than the bigger ones. The smaller ones gave me more freedom to wander around, exploring the town and countryside. In the big towns, like Stuttgart and Cologne, Mom got a little weird about me wandering around alone, which meant I couldn't go see any castles or the other cool stuff (torture museums—'nuff said) without waiting for her to have the time to take me.

There were also a lot more people in the big cities than in the towns. You'd think a lot of people would make for a good place to disappear in, but I'd found that even in a really busy square in Frankfurt or Cologne, surrounded by hundreds of people walking, laughing, talking, kissing . . . even plunked down in the middle of that, I still felt different. I wasn't one of them. I didn't blend in.

GOT FANGS?

"Bullfrogs with big fat warts," I swore as I kicked at the plastic crate behind Elvis's trailer, then went off to see if Imogen was up.

I tapped on the aluminum side of her door and stuck my head in. "You up?"

"Fran! Yes, I'm up. How are you feeling?"

I climbed up the couple of steps into the trailer and sat in the swivel chair across a small round table from her. She was drinking a latte and toying with the remains of a sticky roll.

"Fine." I glanced at the closed door to her bedroom. "Mom wasn't up this morning, but Soren said Ben hauled me out of the main tent last night?"

She sipped at her latte, her face smooth and unreadable. "Yes, he did."

I nodded. I thought the warm blackness that had cloaked me from everyone else had a Ben sort of feel to it. "Did you have fun last night? You looked like the glamour was working overtime on you."

She sighed happily. "It was so wonderful, wasn't it? And Jan—he was the one with all the yummy muscles—was a delight. He has many fine qualities. We went to a club in town after the band ended."

I couldn't help but grin at the wicked look in her eyes. "Sounds like you had even more fun than I imagined. I'm glad you and Jan had a good time. I kind of thought you would after he decked Elvis."

She giggled. "Wasn't that terrible? I should feel sorry about that, but I couldn't help being delighted that Jan knocked him out. Elvis is such a pest about me seeing anyone else, and he's gotten so much worse in the last few weeks."

"He's in looooove," I drawled, making big love-struck cow eyes at her.

"Lust is more like it. I don't think he knows the meaning of the word 'love.' " Imogen set her cup down and gave me an encouraging smile. "Enough about me. You want to tell me about what happened?"

"Last night?" I chewed on my lower lip, trying to think of a way to touch her without her realizing what I was doing, subsequently getting her undies in a bunch because she was officially on my list of suspects. "Um."

She put her hand on my wrist and gave it a little friendly squeeze. "Fran, you don't have to tell me if you don't want to. Friends don't force their friends into divulging secrets."

Friends also don't put their friends on the top of a list of suspected thieves. I squirmed in the chair.

"It's just that I'm worried. Benedikt was very concerned last night; he said you were in a fugue state, and that you'd had some sort of a psychic trauma. I just want you to know that I'm here for you if you need me. We both are. Benedikt cares for you very much, you know."

"Yeah, well, he kind of has to, me being his Beloved and all," I said, utterly and completely miserable. How could I possibly think the thief was Imogen? She was my friend! I liked her. I trusted her. I believed in her.

"Did last night have something to do with your investigation?"

I made another one of those moue faces. "I figured you'd hear about that."

Her eyebrows raised slightly. "Of course I heard about that; I hear about everything. It is true that you agreed to find out who the thief is?"

I nodded, toying with the fingers of my gloves.

"And you're doing that by reading people's intentions when you touch them?"

"Some people," I admitted to my fingers. I hated this, but my back was up against the wall. The only other person on my list was my mother, and I knew, I *knew* she wasn't a thief. Besides the fact that she'd never steal, she wanted the Faire to succeed too badly to do anything to endanger it.

"How many?"

"Seven. Seven people touched the safe." I looked up, trying to dig out my courage from where it had crawled behind my stomach. "Seven people . . . including you."

"Me?" Her eyebrows really went up at that. She looked completely surprised. "I can't imagine when I— Oh, yes. I asked Peter to put something in the safe for me a few weeks ago, and he had me do it."

I blinked a couple of times. It sounded plausible, but at the same time, it sounded awfully darn convenient. "He did? What . . . uh . . . what was it . . . ?"

She smiled. "It was my will."

"Your what?"

"My will. A dispensation of my worldly goods."

"I know what a will is, but geez, Imogen, you're immortal! You're not going to die."

"I can be killed," she said, the faint smile that had been lingering around her lips fading as she traced a finger around the edge of the big latte cup.

"You mean someone wants to kill you, too?"

Okay, the words slipped out without my thinking about them, but as soon as I said them, a weight lifted off my shoulders. Thus far everyone who knew about my curse—Ben, Mom, Imogen, and Soren—thought I had gone back into the main tent last night to find the thief, but the truth was, I had gone specifically to find the person who wanted Ben dead. It was just a hunch that the two people were one and the same.

"Too? What do you mean, 'too'?"

I glanced at the closed door behind her. She froze, her eyes going dark. "Benedikt," she whispered.

"Yeah. That's what I was doing last night. Earlier, when Ben and I were dancing, I felt someone. Someone who was thinking about how much he or she was going to enjoy staking him. Someone really bad."

"Who?" she asked, her voice deep and rough. Her eyes had gone absolutely black now, a shiny, flat black.

"I don't know," I answered, peeling off one set of my gloves. "I wish I knew, I really do, because whoever it is is one sick person."

She looked at the discarded glove on her table, then raised her eyes to mine. The pain in hers was so great, it tainted the air between us. "You wish to touch me. You believe I am guilty."

"Not in wanting Ben dead, no. And not as the thief; it's just that . . . Oh, bullfrogs! I don't know what's what anymore, Imogen. As far as I can tell, no one has stolen the money, but I believe Absinthe and Peter— they don't have it. Which means someone has taken it, either the way a normal thief would, or by . . ."

"Psychic means," she finished, closing her eyes for a

moment. She held out her hand. "I understand. You must do this, if only for your own satisfaction."

"I'm really sorry," I said, hating to eavesdrop on her thoughts. "I'll be quick."

My fingers rested on the pulse point of her wrist. Instantly I was swamped with fear—fear for Ben, fear that the old horrors had started again, fear that she would have to make yet another new life for herself, fear that she would be left alone. Mingled into that was worry about me not accepting who I was, and the role I had to play in Ben's life.

I pulled my fingers back, more than a little shaken by the peek inside her head. "I'm sorry," I said again.

She gave me a smile, a real smile, one filled with understanding and forgiveness, so bright it made the inside of the trailer light up. "It is forgotten. Now, tell me everything about this person you touched. Don't leave anything out."

I didn't. I spilled my guts for a good half hour, telling her everything, from Absinthe's trying to break into my mind, to everyone I had touched, to the dance with Ben . . . It was like she used one of those truth drugs on me, only I *wanted* to tell her everything.

"That's it," I said, wrapping everything up with my few minutes spent with Karl. "That's everyone on my list. I've touched them all, and none of them is the thief. If I can't even find one lousy thief, how am I supposed to find a potential murderer?"

"You didn't touch everyone on the list," Imogen said, her eyes firm on mine. They were back to their original blue, just as blue as the sky outside. "There is one you have not read."

"My mom? I did touch her; I touched her a couple of days ago to find her keys. I would know if she was thinking about taking money—"

"Not your mother . . . Absinthe."

I made a face. "Yeah, well, I eliminated her because it doesn't make any sense for her to make a stink about the money missing. Peter doesn't do the accounts; she does, so he would never have known it had gone missing if she hadn't said something. Besides, I don't think it would be a good idea to touch her. She almost got into my head. . . . If I were touching her while she tried that, I don't think I could keep her out."

"There are ways," she murmured.

"Really? Has she tried it with you?" I couldn't help but be curious. Imogen always seemed so in control, so strong, it was kind of a surprise to know that Absinthe had tried her party tricks on her as well.

"She tries at least once a month." She laughed.

"Really? But . . . you said she already knows about you. Why would she want to get into your head?"

"I have no idea, probably power. She knows who I am, yes, but with that comes the knowledge that should she anger me, I have the means to bring about her destruction."

"You can do that?" I sat in openmouthed surprise. "Then why . . . why . . ."

"Why do I work for the Faire rather than living in a penthouse apartment surrounded by beautiful people and clothes and things, and lots of money?"

I nodded. If someone handed me life on a silver platter, I sure as shooting knew what I'd do with it.

"I've lived that life, Fran. It's amusing for about ten

minutes; then the artificiality of it tarnishes everything. I find that real life, life among mortals, is the only thing that brings me satisfaction. It has brought me such friends as you, after all, and I wouldn't trade your friendship for the most expensive of lifestyles."

"Geez, Imogen," I said, frowning at my fingers, blinking really fast so she wouldn't see the tears. "Just make me cry, why don't you! And after I treated you like a suspect and all . . ."

"You did your job; don't kick yourself for that. Now come, let us put our heads together about this animal who wishes to see Benedikt dead. Tell me again about what you felt when you touched the person."

We spent the next twenty minutes talking over everything I guessed about the person (not much) and everything I had felt in the brief moment of contact (even less). An idea was growing in the back of my mind, just a little niggle of an idea, but the more I tried to look at it, the more it slipped away from me. I gave up on it and turned my attention to stuff I could deal with. We discussed the problem of Absinthe, Imogen insisting that I was going to have to touch her, me swearing to high heaven that I'd rather die than let her know the truth about me.

"She can't hurt you if your mother and I stand behind you—"

"She can, too! Mom'll do anything to stay with the Faire, and that includes selling me into indentured bondage. I don't trust Absinthe one little bit—if she finds out about me, she'll have me doing Fran the Touch Freak acts so fast your head'll spin."

Imogen stood up. "Let us go wake up Benedikt. He

will have some ideas, and since you said you warned him about the attempt on his life, he might have discovered something last night that can help you."

I stood up slowly, not wanting to follow her as she started closing the blinds on the windows. I couldn't deny that he had saved my butt when I was overwhelmed with everyone the night before, but I had my pride. I wasn't going to go running to him every time I had a sticky situation to work out.

"Fran?"

"You know, he probably needs his beauty sleep after last night. And speaking of that, I've got to run along. Since it's our last night here, Mom is holding a circle, and I'm supposed to help her set up for it. She's probably up by now."

"But Fran—what about the investigation? What about Benedikt?"

I paused at the door. "I won't forget; don't worry. I like Ben; I don't want to see him staked. I think . . ." I bit off what I was going to say. There was no way I could put into words the thought bouncing around the back of my head when I couldn't even get a good look at it. "I'll think on it for a while, okay? You, too. If you come up with anything, let me know. I'll see you later."

"You'll see me in an hour, or have you forgotten the children's show?"

"Poop on a stick," I swore. I *had* forgotten. Peter made it a policy that at the end of every stint in towns with a hospital, some of the Faire folk spent a few hours doing magic and illusions for the sick children.

He said it was a good way to promote goodwill and all that, but the truth was that Peter was an old softy, and he just liked cheering up sick kids. "Do you really need me? You can read palms by yourself—"

"You are my apprentice," she pointed out. "That means you have to come with me. It will be for only a few hours, Fran, and we might learn something. Everyone on your list will be there."

There was that. I'd never been on one of the hospital visits, since the thought of sick people gave me the willies, but Mom had gone every time. "Okay. I'll be ready. See you then."

The next hour went pretty quickly. I helped my mother draw a circle on the floor in her tent, setting up the flowers and invocation candles, all while avoiding her questions about what happened last night. She didn't ask very many, which made me believe she and Ben had had a little talk about me while I was passed out, something that made me feel all hot and uncomfortable when I thought about it, so I didn't.

Mom and Imogen and I all rode into town together, following the other cars to a big, ugly green hospital. I kept my hands to myself, afraid of what might be able to seep through the protection of the gloves if I touched anything.

The show for the kids was actually pretty fun. It was all illusion, with just one notable bit of magic that absolutely stopped the show. The kids and nurses and doctors filled one of the big wards, kids in wheelchairs, on regular chairs, propped up on the beds, some even sitting on the floor on big pillows. I figured everyone would be moaning and groaning and near death, but the ward was painted blue and yellow, with brightly colored butterflies scattered around the room. The kids themselves looked pretty cheerful, some of them wearing caps to cover bald heads, others wearing face masks, some in weird contraptions, almost all of them with IVs hooked up to them, but every single one of them had a smile when the show started. I began to see why everyone looked forward to Peter's hospital trips.

Karl and Kurt did a few flashy illusions that had the kids wowed—stuff like turning birdcages with canaries into a big pink rabbit (the rabbit's name was Gertrude, in case you were wondering), making showers of confetti fly out of the unlikeliest of places, pouring milk into some of the kids' hats, only to turn them inside out and show they were dry, that sort of stuff. Mom taught everyone flower-growing spells, and passed out little vials of happiness. Elvis did some card tricks, including one in which he was put into a straitjacket so he couldn't manipulate the cards, and yet he still managed to produce the cards three volunteers had hidden. I felt a little bad about not helping Elvis last night after seeing him do the card tricks—he had a huge bruise under one eye where Jan had socked him. To tell the truth, I was a bit surprised he was part of the show, since I hadn't known he did magic, but the adoring looks he was throwing Imogen explained a lot. No doubt he was there to impress her.

Imogen and I read a few palms, me with my gloves on, trying to do my best to sound upbeat and positive about kids who probably wouldn't have a long life ahead of them. Imogen did a lot better job than me—the kids she read for were laughing by the time she was finished with them.

Peter and Soren's act was the finale of the show, and although most of it was illusion, the last bit Peter did was my favorite example of pure, unadulterated magic. Every time I saw it, it gave me goose bumps, raising the hair on the back of my neck with its simplicity.

"What do I have here?" Peter asked, holding up two eggs, translating his words to Hungarian.

"*Tojások!*" the children cried. "Eggs!"

"Who wants to write their names on the eggs?"

Two dozen hands went up. Soren and Peter walked around, letting a few of the kids sign the eggs with different-colored markers.

"And what happens when you break eggs into a bowl?" Peter cracked both eggs into a clear glass bowl, carefully setting the shells aside. He held the bowl up so everyone could see it, walking along the front row allowing people to look.

"Now, I have here a magic fork! It is magic because it can turn both forward"—he made a clockwise circle with the fork—"and backward."

The fork made a counterclockwise circle.

"When I put the magic fork into the eggs, it scrambles them!"

I rubbed my arms, feeling the goose bumps start. The children watched as Peter whisked the eggs with the fork, giving his standard patter about how magic comes from within each of us, a power that everyone has, but few know how to unlock. Most of the children watched with rapt looks on their faces; a few rolled their eyes as if they knew what would happen.

I smiled to myself. They had *no* idea.

Peter whipped the eggs into an eggy yellow froth, then gave the bowl to Soren to pass around. "What do you get when you beat eggs?" he asked the crowd.

"Scrambled eggs!" the kids yelled back.

"That's right. Has everyone seen? Yes? The eggs are scrambled?"

"Yes," everyone shouted, even the doctors and nurses.

I smiled at Soren. He grinned back at me.

"Ah, but you forget, this is a magic fork! It can work forward . . . and backward."

Peter put the fork in the bowl and began to beat the eggs again . . . in the opposite direction. I rubbed the goose bumps on my arms, watching the kids' eyes grow wider and wider as the eggs began to unscramble themselves. It was magic, pure and simple, and it was wonderful. I understood now why magicians did what they did—the astonishment on the audience's faces was a wonderful thing to behold.

Peter pulled his fork from the bowl, holding it up so everyone could see the two perfectly whole eggs in it. "And now I give the eggs a tap with the magic fork. . . ." Using the two eggshells, he scooped up one whole egg, tapped it with the fork, and handed it to a child he beckoned forward. The kid stared at it with huge eyes while Peter reshelled the second egg, passing that around, too. I knew what everyone who examined the eggs would find—two perfectly whole eggs, signed with the names of the audience. There was no trick, no illusion, no exchange of broken eggs for whole—they were the same eggs, the exact same eggs, broken, scrambled, unscrambled, made whole again.

Magic, huh? Yeah. It's pretty cool.

It's also a heck of a showstopper. Everyone was talking excitedly when we packed up to leave. I know the kids had a good time, but what surprised me was how much fun I had. There I was surrounded by a bunch of children who were just as different as I was, only they were dying because of their differences, and yet none of them asked anyone to use magic to make them better; none of them asked Mom to make the pain go away, or the cancer to disappear, or their blood cells to go back the way they should be. They just laughed and enjoyed, and accepted everything offered.

Mom and Imogen chatted on the way back to the Faire. I let them, trying to figure out what it was that was rattling around the back of my brain. It was something important, something that I saw, but missed seeing, if you know what I mean. Something to do with what was going on, but I couldn't figure out how, or who it concerned, or even why it mattered. It just . . . was.

Chapter Eleven

I tried to pin down the thought later that day, but the last day is always a busy time, usually the busiest night of our stay.

"Hey!" Soren called to me just after lunch. He held up a bridle. "Want to go riding?"

I glanced over at my mother. She was making good-luck amulets. "Do you need me?"

"No, go have some fun. You've worked hard this morning."

I jumped up. She stopped me with a hand on my wrist. "Franny, I want to . . . I want to thank you."

"For what?"

"For joining in. For being part of the Faire. I know you like to think yourself aloof from everyone, but your participation in our new life has meant a lot to me. So . . . thank you."

I mumbled something and escaped, wondering how she could be such a smart witch, and so clueless about me. "I was blackmailed into joining in," I grumbled as I ran out to where Soren was putting a bridle on Bruno. "It's not like I had a choice or anything."

"A choice about what?" he asked as I picked up the bridle he set near Tesla.

"Nothing, doesn't matter. How does this thing work?"

He showed me how to put the bridle on. Tesla wasn't particularly interested in the whole idea, but Soren showed me how to find the spot on Tesla's jaw that I could press to make him open his mouth so I could slide the bit in. We adjusted the straps until the bridle fit; then I jumped onto a rock and climbed onto Tesla's back while Soren held him steady.

"Whoa, big horse," I said, my inner thigh muscles immediately screaming a protest at having to straddle his broad back.

Tesla decided enough was enough; grazing was much more important than standing around with a human on his back. The reins jerked out of my hands, sliding up his neck to his ears as he lowered his head to the ground. I leaned forward to get them, and promptly fell off.

Tesla ignored me.

"You!" I pointed to Soren, who was sitting comfortably on Bruno's back. "Stop laughing. You!" I pointed to Tesla. "Prepare to be ridden. This is war, horse."

It took me three tries, but at last I hoisted myself onto Tesla's back. He wasn't terribly happy about leaving all that lovely grass just waiting to be eaten, but with a few hollered instructions from Soren, we were soon trotting around the big open part of the meadow, where later the cars would park.

"This . . . ow . . . this is . . . *ow* . . . this is a little hard on the . . . ow . . . teeth," I said once I felt safe enough to stop clutching Tesla's mane. "It's a . . . *ow!* . . . bit hard on the thighs, too."

"That's why you need a saddle," Soren said, although I noticed he wasn't grimacing like I was. "Then you can post."

"Post what?"

"Post—it's the way you move to the horse's trot. Makes it easier on your bum."

"Oh. Good. My bum could use easier." I squirmed around a little on Tesla's back, trying to find a comfortable position, my legs tightening on him as I tried to shift off his hard backbone. All of a sudden his head came up and his neck arched as he shifted into another gear. I know, I know, horses don't have gears, but he went from moving like he was on a road filled with potholes to one that was newly paved. His trot smoothed out so I was hardly jarred at all as he kind of floated along the ground with long, sweeping strides. I kept my legs tight around his sides, unsure of what had happened, but appreciating the new gait.

"What are you doing?" Soren yelled. I looked back. He was stopped, his mouth hanging open in surprise.

"Darned if I know," I yelled back, and eased up on the reins. "Whatever it is, I like it!"

Tesla did the smooth, flowing trot in a big wide circle around Soren and Bruno, then stumbled over a hole, regained his feet, and came to an abrupt stop as he did so.

I, of course, promptly fell off again.

"How did you do that?" Soren asked as he rode up. I stood up, rubbing my butt. Just my luck—I had landed right on a rock. "How did you make him move like that?"

I grabbed the reins and started walking back toward the small area where the horses grazed. "I told you, I don't know. It's something Tesla did by himself."

"I've seen that before," Soren said, more to himself than to me. "On TV. Horse trials. Dressage, it's called."

"Whatever. I think I've had enough riding for— Oh, hey, look, it's Panna! That's the girl whose grandfather owned Tesla," I explained to Soren.

I led Tesla over to Panna, who greeted him with teary eyes. (No surprise there; I had her number now. She was a puddler—the type who puddled up at anything.) "Hi, Panna. I was starting to think you wouldn't be able to come by."

"Hello, Fran. Hello, Tesla. You were riding him."

"You saw us? Yeah, we were trotting. The vet said that a little exercise is good for him, as long as I didn't push him too far. This is my friend Soren."

Soren said hi, then took Bruno off to be groomed for the evening's show. Panna patted Tesla, gave him an apple, and chatted happily about how her grandfather used to let her ride him when she was a little girl.

"You want to ride him for a little bit? I don't think he'd mind. We didn't do too much."

She smoothed down her cute blue-and-white sundress. "No, thank you. I am not dressed for the riding."

I looked down at my scruffy cutoff shorts and faded purple T-shirt with horse slobber on it, and decided it was better if I didn't say anything.

"Tesla looks happy, doesn't he?" She moved around to stroke his velvety-soft nose, giggling when his whiskers tickled her hands. "I am so glad you bought him. He will be happy with you."

"I think so. I hope so. He's eating enough, and the vet says he's in good shape. Hey, while I'm thinking of it, what did your grandfather tell you about Tesla?"

She stroked the long curve of his neck. Tesla, I had come to realize, was a big ham who ate up attention like that. He'd nod his head whenever someone stopped petting him, watching you with those big, huge brown eyes that always seemed to be secretly laughing. "What did Grandfather tell me? Nothing other than that Tesla was special, very special."

I flicked a piece of grass off his mane. "Special, how? Special, smart? Special, fast like a racehorse?"

Her shoulders rose and fell in a shrug. "Grandfather did not say. He just said *alkalmi*. Special."

"Huh." I traced the L on Tesla's cheek. "Do you know what a Lipizzan is?"

She shook her head.

"Hmm. I don't know anything about them, either, other than that a friend of mine thinks Tesla is one. Guess I'll have to ask him just what one is."

Panna chatted for a little longer, then waved when a girl a little older than me called for her. "That's my sister, Jolan. She's coming to the Faire tonight, but says I can't because I'm too young. I don't think I'm too young, do you?"

"How old are you?"

"Thirteen."

"Um . . ." I thought of the piercing tent, the dungeon room, the people crammed together dancing under the influence of the glamour. I might be only sixteen, but I sure felt a gazillion years older than her. "You know, it might be better if you waited until we come back next year."

She made a little pout, but didn't have time to argue. Instead she pressed a slip of paper into my hand. "It is my address. You will write to me. I like to have a pen pal with you."

"Sure thing," I said. "I'll let you know how Tesla's doing, okay?"

"Okay," she said; then her eyes filled with tears (again) and she hugged Tesla, hugged me, and ran off wiping her eyes.

I spent the next hour grooming Tesla, ate a quick dinner with Mom, Peter, Soren, and Imogen, then changed into my Gypsy wear for the evening. Imogen said I looked very mysterious in the skirt and blouse, and that people who had me read their palms would be more inclined to believe me if I looked the part.

"That's stupid," I groused as I accepted the book on palmistry that she'd forced on me. "I could do an absolutely perfect reading wearing my jammies and bathrobe as long I was touching them, but no one will believe me unless I look like Esmeralda the Gypsy Vixen?"

"Not Esmeralda," Imogen said as she tipped her head and eyed me when I presented my Gypsy-clad self to her for inspection. "Francesca the enigmatic. With your lovely dark hair and eyes, you very much look the part. The customers will adore you."

"Yeah, right," I said, not believing a word. I glanced

toward the windows. The sun was going down, the sky streaked with the familiar peach and orange and brilliant red. "So . . . um . . . when does Ben get up?"

She smiled a "you like my brother, don't you?" smile at me. "If we closed the blinds, he could come out of the bedroom now. Would you like me to see if he's awake?"

"Naw," I said. "It's not important. Maybe I'll see him later."

"Don't forget the book!"

I made a face but grabbed it, waving as I toddled out the door. Mom wanted to introduce me to some of her Wiccan friends, so I made a brief appearance in our trailer, where everyone was gathered for precircle munchies. Mom held circles about once a month and often on the last night we were in a town, when she knew there would be a lot of witches to form a circle powerful enough to have an effect.

Okay, word to those of you who are at this very moment freaking out—just like everything else in this world, there are good witches and bad ones. Some call themselves Wiccans; some call themselves priestesses of the Goddess. They're all basically the same—witches. My mother, of course, practiced good magic—earth magic, they call it. Pagans are very big on that sort of thing. When she and her fellow witches/Wiccans/whatever get together, they hold circles to practice their magic. A witch by herself can do limited magic, but a circle . . . Well, let me just say that you don't ever want to go up against a circle if you've done something bad. There was a guy in Oregon, one of those religious-rights guys who thought all witches were bad and should be put in jail (or worse), who started physically attacking local witches. Mom and her gang formed a circle and took care of him pretty quickly.

I heard he still walks backward, seven months later.

So I did the meet-and-greet thing, smiled at all the Hungarian witches, and took myself off before they all wanted to start doing blessings on me (Mom's group is very big on blessings). As I was leaving, one of the witches—an older woman with tiny gray curls and really big, chunky jewelry—suddenly tensed and sniffed the air just like one of those hunting dogs does when it sees a bird.

She rattled off something to Mom, who looked confused. Mom's friend Zizi, who'd come in from Germany, translated for her. "She says she smells something foul."

"That would be Davide. He gets gas when he eats too much fish," I said.

Davide shot me a look that would have killed a normal person.

Everyone else ignored my little joke. The big jewelry woman said something else. Zizi's eyes got big as everyone in the trailer fell silent. "Bella says what she smells is unclean."

Unclean? I don't think she was talking about someone missing their morning shower. I glanced at Mom. She was looking very worried. "Unclean how, Zizi? Unclean as in impure, or unclean as in"—Mom waved her hand around—"damned?"

Bella made a show of sniffing the air again. "*Kárho-zott*," she said.

Everyone gasped.

"Damned," Zizi whispered.

"Erp," I said. And meant it.

"What are you doing?"

I stopped sniffing the air and turned. Ben was leaning against one of the posts holding the main tent up. "Trying to find something damned. You look gorgeous, as usual. You've probably never have a bad hair day in your whole life, have you? I bet you've never even had pimples. You're too handsome for pimples; they're probably afraid to come near you."

One ebony eyebrow zoomed upward. "Thank you. I think. You look . . . nice."

I crossed my arms. I looked as good as I was going to get, and we both knew it. "Nice? Just nice? I was lovely the other night."

"Yes, you were, but then I'd never seen you in 'girl stuff' before, and now I have."

My nostrils—of their own accord, I'll have you know—flared in anger. "Well, too bad, so sad; this is it as far as my girl stuff goes."

He smiled one of his wicked smiles, the one that makes me forget that I don't want a boyfriend, especially one who thinks of relationships in terms of centuries. "I have something for you."

I looked at what he held out to me. "That's a ring."

"It is."

"It's pretty."

"I like it. I hope you will, too."

I took a step forward and peered into his hand. "What kind of a stone is that?"

"A ruby."

"Oh. Those are kind of expensive, aren't they?"

His hand never wavered. The ring sitting on his palm glowed a warm red at me. The stone was set into a dark gold band, words in a fancy script wrapping around it.

"That's the same as the tattoo you have."

"Yes, it is. Are you going to take it?"

I kept my arms crossed and considered him. "That depends. It looks old. Did it belong to someone else?"

"Yes. My mother. I want you to have it, Fran. The ring won't give you any pain, I promise you."

Of its own volition, my hand reached out to take it. It was heavy and warm, a soothing warmth. A woman's face flashed before my eyes, her hair dark like Ben's, a laughing woman, a happy woman. "Your mother was pretty."

"I thought she was."

I kept my eyes on his, the ring pulsing with remembered life in my hand. "She loved your father very much."

He said nothing, just watched me.

"But she died. I thought Moravians were immortal?"

"They are. My mother wasn't a Moravian."

I glanced down at the ring. I liked it. It was nice. He was right: touching it didn't bring me any pain. "She wasn't your father's Beloved?"

"If she was, I wouldn't be what I am."

"Huh?"

He stepped forward, taking the ring from my left hand, sliding it over my thumb, then over my forefinger, then over my middle finger, where he left it. The ring grew warmer for a second, then tightened around my finger until it fit securely. "*Now* you look lovely. Dark Ones who find their Beloveds are redeemed. Their sons aren't born bearing the sin of their fathers."

"Oh, I see. But your mom loved your dad. How could she do that if she wasn't his Beloved?"

A flash of pain darkened his eyes for a second. "I couldn't tell you why; I know only what was. She loved him. And she was happy with him. She would want you to have this ring."

I looked down at my hand where the ring sat. It felt right, like it was meant to be there. "This doesn't mean we're engaged or anything, right? That weird finger thing you just did isn't some strange Moravian ceremony, is it? 'Cause if it is, I can't keep it."

"No, it doesn't mean we're engaged."

You'll notice he didn't answer my second question. I noticed, too. "It doesn't mean we're dating?"

"Nor dating."

"A friendship ring, that's all it is, right?"

He tucked my hair behind my ear. I decided not to push the point. He leaned forward, just a smidge, just a tiny little lean forward.

"Are you going to kiss me?" I asked, unable to keep my mouth from blurting out everything I thought.

"Do you want me to?" he asked, his breath fanning my face.

My inner Fran started turning cartwheels of joy. I told her to take a Valium and call me in the morning. "Yes. No. I'm not sure. What was the question?"

GOT FANGS?

He leaned forward another smidge. Inner Fran threw a party, complete with balloon animals and ice-cream sundaes.

His lips were warm and soft on mine, teasing me, begging me to accept them, to caress them, to yield to their seductive heat. He kissed me until my head started to swim; then when he was done kissing me, he held me up while I tried to get my legs to support me.

"Boy, you sure can learn a lot about kissing in three hundred and twelve years," I said once I got my breath back.

He smiled. It was one of those smug male smiles, but I let him get away with it. Any guy who kissed like he did deserved to be a little bit smug.

"What happens to your fangs?" I asked. "Oh, geez, I didn't say that out loud, did I?"

His lips quirked. "Yes, you did."

"I'm sorry. I'm an idiot today. You'll have to forgive me; I'm not normally such a boob." I glanced up at him. "Um. What does happen to them?"

"What happens to them when?"

"You know, when you're not using them. Do they fold back like a snake's? Do they pop up into your gums? Do they grow when you need them?"

"Does it really matter?"

"No, I suppose not. I just kind of wondered."

"When I need them, they're there. Does that answer your question?"

"Not really, no, but I suppose it would be rude to push it, huh?"

His look said it would. "I have a question for you: what were you trying to accomplish last night?"

"In the crowd, you mean?" He nodded. I took a couple of steps away, just because inner Fran gets all swoony when she is too close to him. "Ah. I kind of figured you'd ask about that. You got a few minutes?"

"As many as you need."

I told him about the deal I had made with my mother and Absinthe. I didn't, however, explicitly tell him I was thief hunting in the main tent. I decided that if he couldn't lie to me, it wasn't nice of me to lie to him. So I just *implied* that I was thief hunting.

Unfortunately, Ben wasn't stupid. "You were looking for the thief when you returned to the main tent last night?"

I tried on his silence policy to see how it felt.

"Fran, what were you doing in the main tent last night?"

Guess I didn't do it quite right. I gave a little sigh. "I think the thief and person who wants to kill you are the same person. I was looking for him. Or her. Whichever."

His eyes went absolutely black—not a shiny black like when he kisses me, but a majorly annoyed, ticked-off, so-black-no-light-escaped-from-them black. "You were trying to find the person who wants me dead."

I turned my back on him and strolled off a few steps, looking up at the stars like I didn't have a really pissed-off vampire behind me. "Maybe."

The pissed-off vampire was in front of me all of a sudden, moving so fast I couldn't see him, his hands hard on my arms. "You are *not* to protect me, Fran. That's my duty."

I squirmed out of his grip. "Look, you may think

160

there's something between us, but there's not. And if there were, I didn't agree to it, got that? So you can just cut out all of this macho bull about big strong you protecting weak little me. In case you haven't noticed, I'm neither little nor weak. I can solve my own problems. I can take care of myself."

"You don't know what you're talking about—" he started to say.

I interrupted him. "Oh, so now I'm stupid as well as being weak? Thanks, Ben. No, really, thanks bunches."

I turned and walked in the other direction. His voice stung my back like a lash, making me stop. "You *are* weak, Fran, weak when it comes to the dark powers and those who use them. You have *no* concept of how dangerous this person is. Whether or not you like it, we are bound together, and I will protect you as best I can, and that includes making you stop this investigation into the thefts."

"Ha!" I marched back to where he stood all stiff and glowering. One part of my mind—the inner-Fran part—was swooning to herself about how powerful and deadly he looked; the other part—the sane part—commented to itself that it was odd that no matter how menacing Ben was, I felt perfectly safe with him. "You can't make me stop anything, fang boy! I made a deal with my mother and Absinthe to investigate, and that's just what I'm going to do."

"You'll get yourself killed . . . or worse."

"There's nothing worse than death, except maybe having to go through the tenth grade again."

He didn't even bat an eyelash at my joke. *Men!*

"You have no idea of the dangers in this world, Fran. You don't even have the most basic, rudimentary protection skills, skills your mother should have taught you."

I shoved his shoulder. He didn't budge, not an inch. It was like he was made of rock or something. "No one picks on my mom but me, got that? She hasn't done anything wrong."

His eyes all but spat black at me. "She didn't even teach you how to guard your mind against others! That is the most basic skill, and yet you didn't know it. You know no protection wards, no ways to keep yourself from harm when facing someone more powerful than you—"

"Mom doesn't know how to do wards! She asked Imogen about them, but *your* sister wouldn't tell her how to do it. How can she teach me something that she doesn't know?" Now he was really ticking me off. I admit I was curious about Mom's not telling me how to guard my mind, but she probably didn't know there was such a thing.

"Then *I'll* show you!" he yelled at me.

"Fine!" I bellowed back at him.

We both stood there glaring at each other, breathing a little hard because of our fight.

He closed his eyes for a second, then opened them. The weren't quite as black as they were before. He touched my cheek, just a little butterfly touch, but I felt it all the way to my toes. "I can't lose you, Fran. If anything happened to you—"

I smacked his hand away. "What's the ward, tough guy?"

He showed me. When you draw a ward, you follow a basic pattern, but each person makes a little change to it, something unique that only he or she knows. Ben watched me draw the basic ward, then told me to add something else, another little bit that was all my own. I tried a few curves, a few extra swoops in the middle. He made me do the customized ward over and over again until I had it memorized.

My inner Fran pointed out that the customized bit was his name, written in cursive. I told her to get a life.

"Try it again," he snapped, still obviously peeved with me. That was fine with me, because I was still annoyed with his Mr. Protecto attitude. "You're still not doing it right."

"I am so! I'm drawing it the exact same way!"

"You have to believe in the power of the ward, in your ability to draw it. Without that you're just waving your finger around in the air."

I felt like screaming at him. Goddess above, was there anyone so annoying as a pushy vamp? "I'm trying, okay! So get off my back!"

"Do it again!" he snarled.

"Fine, I will. And then you know what? I am *so* leaving you! I never want to see you again, got that? *Never!*" I threw everything I had at the ward, all my emotions, all my thoughts, all my will, every last bit of desire I felt to go home and crawl back into my nice, safe little world. As I traced the last symbol, the last curve, the ward flared to life in the air between us, an intricate gold pattern that slowly dissolved particle by particle into nothing.

The ward was drawn. I was protected.

"Happy?" I snapped.

"Not even remotely," he growled.

"Noogies of toughness," I said through my teeth, and walked away.

"Where are you going?" he yelled after me.

"To do my job!" I yelled back, and stormed off toward the bright lights of the Faire.

Chapter Twelve

Yeah, okay, so you saw through my big act. The truth was, I was so angry at Ben and his "you will stop investigating this because you are a girl and I am a vamp" attitude, I ran off without asking for his help, which I had finally decided I would do, because honestly, what is the good in having a tame vampire around unless you put him to use once in a while?

So there I was, marching down the length of the Faire looking really mean and all, when inside I was wondering just how the heck I was going to tackle Absinthe without a little help from my friends (namely Ben). I was so focused on yelling at myself—and thinking of at least a dozen really cool responses to Ben's snarky comments—that I ran right into Imogen before I saw her.

"Fran, I'm sorry; I didn't see you." Evidently I wasn't the only one walking around all introspective. Imogen looked mad enough to kill, her blue eyes all sparkly with anger. She held a crumpled-up bit of paper in her hand. "Have you seen Benedikt?"

"Yeah, just a few minutes ago, over by the main tent. What's the matter? You look really cheesed about something."

"I *am* cheesed; I am so very cheesed you could call me Gouda." She shoved the paper into my hands. "Read that. Have you ever read anything so ridiculous in your life? The nerve of him!"

I smoothed out the paper and read the short type-written note. *My beloved Imogen,* it started. I glanced down to see who had signed it (Elvis), then looked up. "Um . . . do you really want me to read your love letter?"

"It's not a love letter," she said, grinding her teeth over the words.

Ouch. I read the letter aloud. " 'My beloved Imogen, long have I waited for you to realize that I am the one man life has fated for you, but time and time again you insist on flaunting your infidelities before me. This will end, tonight, once and for all. You will meet me at the bus stop to Kapuvár at midnight.' The bus stop? Oh, the one down the road from here. That's close to where I found Tesla. 'From there we will go into town and be married at once. You are mine, Imogen, and I no longer intend to share your charms. Your devoted Elvis.' Boy, what a maroon. What is it with these guys and their bossy ways?"

"He is insane, that is what he is, insane! I am *not* his, and he is *not* the man fated for me, and I will have Benedikt tell him so in a way that will guarantee that Elvis will not bother me again."

I looked down at the paper in my bare hand. The

letter was typewritten, so it didn't hold as much emotion as one that was handwritten might, but even so I could feel Elvis's determination to have Imogen. I gave it back to her. "Yeah, well, I suppose Ben could put the fear of the Goddess into Elvis."

"It is not the Goddess that Elvis shall be fearing when Benedikt is finished with him," Imogen said dramatically, shaking back her mane of blond hair. She looked different somehow, more intense, more . . . just more. I guess it was because I'd never truly seen her angry before that I was impressed by her fury. "I shall send him to this little rendezvous. My brother is very protective of those he loves. Elvis will soon learn just how unwise it is to cross a Moravian."

I pursed my lips as she thanked me, and strode off down the long aisle, her hair streaming behind her, righteous indignation pouring from her in waves. I almost felt sorry for Elvis . . . almost.

"Like you have any sympathy to spare for anyone else when you've got the mother of all mind readers to grill?" I asked myself, then reluctantly turned toward the small kiosk where I knew Absinthe would be setting up for ticket sales.

I found her just leaving the kiosk, giving Tess, the ticket girl, some last-minute instructions. I watched her for a minute, trying to steel my nerves to touch her. I put my lace gloves on over my bare hands so she wouldn't notice anything different about me, reminding myself that I was protected by my ward and could keep Absinthe out of my head (I hoped) if she tried to get in. I had faith in the ward—I knew Ben wouldn't lead me astray with it—but am not too ashamed to admit that my faith in my mental No Trespassing sign was a bit shaky when it came to being physically in contact with Absinthe.

"You can do this, Fran," I whispered to myself, moving out of the shadow so Absinthe would see me when she turned around. "It's just one person, one last person. She can't hurt you."

Absinthe turned and started toward me. Inner Fran screamed and urged me to run away. Outer Fran forced a smile and tried to look like she wasn't going to barf. "Hi, Absinthe. I have a quick question for you, if you've got a mo'."

"A mo'?" She stopped, frowning as she scanned beyond me. She normally made the rounds just before the Faire opened to make sure everyone was where they were supposed to be.

"Moment."

"Ah. Are you not assisting Imogen vith the reading of the palms? Vy is it you are not at her tent?"

"There's still fifteen minutes." I chewed on my lip for a second, sizing Absinthe up. Really, she was a tiny thing, tinier than Imogen, but you forgot about that because her personality was so big, if you know what I mean. Her spiky pink hair helped, too. Besides, there's nothing like the knowledge that someone can bring you to your knees with just a flex of their psychic powers to make you respect them. I tried once more to pin down the fleeting feeling that I had seen something today that was important, something that I should have noticed, something someone said or did, but there were too many vague "somethings" to be of any help. I took a deep breath. "It's about the safe. You said that the morning after it was stolen the door was locked? You're sure it wasn't propped open?"

"No, it vas closed. Vat sort of a fool are you thinking I am?"

"Sorry, I didn't mean to imply anything; I just thought I'd better check."

"You have found nothing, *ja?*" She *tsk*ed, and started to walk past me. "That is because it vas that Josef who is the thief. I vill find him, you vill see, and ven I do—"

Desperate to touch her before she walked off, I said loudly, "Oh, you have a big bug on you," just as I brushed my hand across her shoulder.

She stopped and spun around, her eyes wide and almost glowing. "You." She gasped. I snatched my hand back, mentally slamming shut the stainless-steel doors of my sealed room, just barely closing my mind to her before she got in. I could feel her nudging around the edges, pushing at the walls, trying to find a way in, but I kept the mental image of my sealed room solid, and thank the Goddess, both it and the ward worked.

She swayed for a moment as if she were suddenly weak; then her chin snapped up and she leveled a pale blue gaze at me that made me take a couple of steps back. "I am not finished with you," she hissed, turning on her heel to stomp off.

"Holy moly," I breathed, rubbing my arms. They were all goose bumpy, like they got around real magic, only these weren't goose bumps of fun. They were scared-silly goose bumps.

Imogen ran past, stopped to have a word with Absinthe, then beckoned me toward her tent. I followed more slowly, trying to fit together everything I knew. Absinthe wasn't the thief. She had more power than I had imagined, but she wasn't a thief. She honestly thought Josef, the lead guitarist, had taken it. Which meant I had seven suspects, all of whom *weren't* the thief. In other words, I was back to square one.

We were busy for the next three hours, just as I knew we would be. Last nights are always packed, since the Faire comes around only every year to year and a half. I more or less handled all the palm reading (with both sets of gloves on, in case you were wondering) while Imogen read runes. I didn't even have time to ask Imogen whether she found Ben, and what he thought of Elvis's letter, let alone try to figure out what I was going to do about my failed investigation.

Just before midnight it started to rain bullfrogs. And no, I'm not speaking metaphorically.

"What the . . . That's a frog," Imogen said as a big lumpy green-and-yellow frog jumped onto her table, blinked at her a couple of times, then jumped off.

"Not just a frog, a bullfrog," I said, then stood up and hurried toward the front of the tent when I heard shrieking. People were yelling and holding things over their heads as they raced for cover. "Bullfrogs aren't good. I'm going to go check on my mom. I'll be back in a minute."

I raced out of the tent, trying to avoid bumping into people or stepping on the frogs that were falling out of the sky. Luckily the frogs were pretty quick on their feet, because I didn't see any of them smooshed as people ran through them. I saw a lot of them bounce when they hit the ground, though, and I have to say, they looked as surprised to see me as I was to see them.

"Mom? It's raining bullfrogs!" I yelled as I pushed past the people who were hiding under the opening of the tent. Because of the circle, the rest of the tent had been emptied of its usual table, chairs, etc. My mother and the rest of the witches had closed the circle and were all standing with their eyes closed, swaying slightly as someone chanted the invocation to the Goddess . . . standard circle stuff. I knew better than to cross into the circle (I did that once—it took three weeks before my eyebrows grew back), so I skirted around the circle until I could tug on the back of Mom's dress.

"Bullfrogs," I whispered. She opened one eye and let it glare at me.

"No, seriously, it's raining bullfrogs. Outside."

"It is a plague," the woman standing next to her said without opening her eyes.

"It is?"

"I know about the frogs, Fran," Mom whispered, shooing me away. "Now go on; we're trying to focus our energy on identifying the unholy one that has brought them here."

Wonderful. Something unholy was causing bull-frogs to rain down on the Faire. Could my life *get* any stranger?

A man in a blue-and-red-sequined jumpsuit with a gold lamé shoulder cape walked by, pausing to do a hip shake when he saw me.

Well, I guess that answered my question.

"Hey, there, little lady. You're looking mighty fine to the King, yes, you are. Would you be looking for someone to dance with?"

"Um . . . no, not really. Have you . . . uh . . . noticed the frogs, Elvis?"

He looked around him. "Now that you mention it, there are an awful lot of the little buggers. Loud things, frogs. Don't like 'em, uh-huh."

Evidently the rain of bullfrogs was ending, because only one or two more fell. The last few on the ground hopped around with loud croaks, heading off into the darkness. I hoped they all found the stream before they got squashed by cars.

"Right. Well, if you'll excuse me." I started past Elvis back toward Imogen's tent, then paused, twisting the ring Ben had given me, something making my inner Fran stand up and shout.

"Suit yourself," Elvis said as he headed toward the main tent. I glanced at my watch. It was two minutes to midnight. How could Elvis be here if he intended to meet Imogen in two minutes at a bus stop almost a kilometer down the road? And where was Ben?

"Hey, Elvis?" I ran after him, careful not to touch him when he swung around toward me. "Are you going to watch the band?"

"Sure am, little filly. You want to dance with me after all?"

"No, I can't; I have something to do. I just thought . . . uh . . . I thought Imogen said she was meeting you somewhere. Somewhere else." Lame, yes, but it was the best I could do, given the circumstances.

He looked puzzled, and scratched his big, poofy black 'do. "Meet Imogen? Nope, don't have any plans to go anywhere else, just the main tent. I'll see her there. You sure you don't wanna dance with the King?" He did a few swivel-hip moves. "I'm pretty good!"

"No, thanks, I've got something to do. See you."

Other than the psychometric thing, I've never been psychic—not ever, nothing, *nada*. But all of a sudden, as Elvis walked off to the main tent, I knew that something was terribly, horribly, massively wrong. Little tiny bits of things started to come together in my brain, just like a jigsaw puzzle.

Elvis wrote that note to Imogen; I knew it, I felt it.

Elvis was obsessed with her; everyone knew that. I had felt it, too.

Elvis probably wouldn't like a brother who had the power to make him leave Imogen alone. He might even go so far as to want to hurt that brother.

Elvis was a demonologist. Demons were bad news, impure beings, unholy. *Damned*. Their appearance was usually heralded by a physical manifestation, something like . . .

"Bullfrogs!" I raced back toward Imogen's booth. She was putting everything into her bag, chatting casually with a lingering customer.

"Where's Ben?" I yelled as soon as I got within shouting distance.

"Benedikt?" Imogen glanced toward the guy who was chatting with her. "He's gone to take care of the little matter I mentioned earlier."

"It's a trap," I yelled, and veered off to the left. "Elvis is here, but it's raining bullfrogs."

She frowned as I dashed by her. "Fran, what are you talking—"

"*Demon!*" I yelled over my shoulder, and raced around the nearest trailer to where Tesla and Bruno were hobbled. My fingers shook, slipping off the leather buckles as I tried to unhook the hobble. Tesla nosed my head as I bent over his feet. I ripped my gloves off, tearing at the leather straps until they gave way.

"Come on, old boy, we have to go warn Ben that it's a trap." I snapped the lead rope onto Tesla's halter, swinging it over his neck to tie it into a kind of bridle. I led him over to a crate, lunging onto his back. "C'mon, c'mon, c'mon," I urged, tapping him with my heels like Soren had taught me.

Tesla trotted through the trailers, weaving through the long black shadows cast in the light of the big lamps until suddenly we were past the edge of the Faire. A long, sloping length of ground stretched toward the road. I wrapped Tesla's mane around my hands and dug my heels in, shouting encouragement. He took off, his speed surprising me. I guess he wasn't as old as everyone thought.

The ride to the bus stop is a bit of a nightmare in my memory—although the moon was out, there wasn't a lot of light to see by, and cars were heading toward the Faire, not away from it, so that their headlights blinded us. I remembered that the vet said I couldn't ride Tesla on the pavement until he had shoes, so I kept him to the soft grass shoulder. Even so, he stumbled in the dark a couple of times. I leaned low over

his neck, both hands tangled in his mane as he gal-
loped along, his breath growing louder and louder until it matched the refrain of *Please be all right, please
be all right* that was chanting in my head. We took a
couple of shortcuts through some front yards, but I
don't think we trampled too many flower beds. We
raced past cars, dogs, houses, other horses . . . all of it
was a blur as Tesla's legs pounded the ground in a
rhythm that was etched into my brain. *Please be all
right, please be all right. . . .*

By the time we rounded the corner a short distance
away from the stop, Tesla was sounding like a freight
train, his breathing a winded roar. My hands were
cramped from clinging to his lead rope and mane, my
legs shaking with fear and strain as they clung to his
heaving sides. Up ahead on the road, next to a big
open pasture, a lone street lamp lit a wooden sign
marked with an A (for autobus).

"Ben?" I yelled, pulling back on the makeshift reins.
Tesla slowed down to a painful trot, then stopped, his
head hanging down. "Ben? Are you here?"

There was nothing to be seen, no Ben, no cars, no
houses even. Just a lonely stretch of road with a bus
stop sign. Maybe I was wrong; maybe I'd gotten
everything wrong. Maybe Elvis wasn't the one who
wanted Ben dead—

Tesla gave an ugly scream, a sound I hope I never
hear again, his front end rising up in the classic horse-
standing-on-back-legs pose you see in statues. I
yelped and grabbed his neck, wrapping my arms
around it as his front legs slashed out, but I lost my

grip anyway and ended up going sideways, off Tesla and onto the ground next to him.

In front of us, a black, horrible shadow gathered itself, then formed into a man. That is, it looked like a man—it had two eyes, two ears, a nose and mouth, all that stuff—but I had to blink a couple of times as I got to my feet to make sure I was seeing what I thought I was seeing. As soon as the stench hit me, I knew it for what it was.

Demon.

"Holy cow," I breathed, then jumped to attention as the demon turned toward us. My ward suddenly glowed to life, but not gold like when I drew it; this time it was black, a heavy, ominous black that seemed to scream into the night.

The demon shrieked and jumped back as if it had been stung. Two bullfrogs fell from the sky. The demon snarled something that just *felt* bad, and turned its eyes to Tesla, who was snorting like mad, alternating pawing at the ground and rising up to slash the air with his front feet. The demon didn't seem to like Tesla, either, and backed up a couple more steps.

Okay, now here's the thing—I know nothing about demons, not one single thing. Except that they're bad news. But here I had one standing there more or less looking me in the face, and I didn't have the slightest clue about what to do to stop it, or how to make it tell me what it had done to Ben, or even how to destroy it. I was helpless, clueless, and for the first time in my life, I wished I had paid attention when Mom tried to teach me all of her witchy stuff.

I wanted to run screaming into the night, but Ben's life was at stake. I had made a big deal about being able to take care of my problems, so I figured I'd better do just that. "What have you done with the Dark One?" I yelled at the demon.

It laughed at me, a nasty, hissing sort of laugh that had two more bullfrogs and a surprised-looking snake falling from the sky. "You have no power over me, mortal."

Its voice was awful, like an amplified screech of fingernails on a blackboard. Tesla rose up again, his front hooves slashing through the air. The demon jumped backward.

When in doubt, freak 'em out. I threw my left hand into the air like Mom does when she's calling on the spirits. "I am Francesca. I wield a far greater power than you will ever know, demon. Answer me—what have you done to the Dark One you were sent to destroy?"

It snickered again (more snakes and a couple of what I think were eels dropped onto the ground behind it), slowly walking a big circle around me and Tesla. My ward flared black again, and I turned to keep it between me and the demon. "You wield no power, mortal. I do not fear you. The one you seek is beyond your help." It nodded its head toward the field behind me. "Go and find him if you like; my work is finished."

While it was speaking I was aware of the two round lights from a car coming from the Faire growing brighter and brighter. The demon's back was to the car, though, and evidently it was too busy taunting me to hear the engine until it was too late. As the headlights finally hit it, it spun around. The car didn't even slow down; it just ran the demon over. I jumped for the pasture, yanking Tesla off the shoulder. Although I heard the car squeal to a stop, I didn't hesitate. I ran out into the blackness of the field, guided by a horrible pain in my heart to where I knew Ben was lying dead.

I had killed him. If only I had figured out what was going on before it was too late . . . but I hadn't, and now he was dead. Gone. I'd never see him again.

I almost stepped on him because I couldn't see through the tears. His body was crumpled up next to a small shrub, his jacket half off, a huge, bloody, gaping hole in his chest. "Oh, Goddess, no!" I yelled, and grabbed Ben's head, holding him with one arm as I tried to slow the bleeding in his chest. "Please, no, oh, Ben, no!"

The demon shrieked again, an angry shriek, one that promised pain and retribution and all sorts of revenge that I couldn't even imagine. I ignored it. "Ben, please don't die. Please. I'm so sorry for what I said. I won't leave you; I swear it."

A white shape blurred at the edge of my vision. I looked up, expecting to see Tesla, but it was Imogen. Tears blurred my eyes as I clutched Ben's lifeless body. "He's dead, Imogen. The demon killed him and it's all my fault. I should have known it was Elvis. I should have known what was happening. He's dead because of me."

"He's not dead," Imogen said, falling to her knees beside us. "I would know if he were dead, and he's not." She put her hands over the huge hole in his chest, the one that blood was still sluggishly dripping out of. "You have to help him, Fran. I can't heal him and anchor him at the same time. You have to help."

"Help him? Help him how? I don't know what to do about a demon—"

"Don't worry about that; I broke its legs and pierced its heart with silver. It won't be going very far."

I stared at my hands, which were covered in Ben's blood, hearing the words, but not understanding them. "How . . . how do I help Ben?"

"You're his Beloved; you're the only one who can reach him. Merge with him, join your mind to his, and hold on to him, bring him back to us. Don't let him go."

"I don't know how to merge with him! I've never done anything like this! I don't know what to do."

"Only you can do it, Fran. Only you." Tears streaked down her face as she closed her eyes, murmuring words over him in a language I didn't understand. I looked down at Ben's face, that handsome, wonderful face, and knew that if I did what Imogen wanted, it would bind me to Ben in a way that would never leave me free from him. I wouldn't just be Fran the weirdo who could tell things by touching them; I'd be Fran the Beloved, and if I thought I'd had a hard time fitting in before, I imagine being the immortal girlfriend of a vampire would just about make blending into the crowd impossible. It was Ben or me; the decision was that simple.

I put my hands on either side of his face and mentally opened up the door to my safe room.

Ben? Are you there? It's me, Fran. Imogen's here, too. She's trying to fix the hole in your chest so you won't die. I don't want you to die, Ben. Can you hear me?

There was silence. No sense of him filled my head. It was like he wasn't there.

Ben?

"He's not answering," I said, not caring that the tears were rolling down my face, too. "He's not there."

"He's there; you just have to find him," Imogen said, lifting her head. Her eyes were filled with so much pain that it hurt to look at her. "Please, Fran. Please save my brother."

I can't, my inner Fran cried out. *I'm just me; I can't do any of this. I don't have any power, not really, nothing useful. I can't save him!*

You already have, a soft voice echoed in my head.

I sobbed his name out loud. *You're not dead? Please, Ben, tell me you're not dead.*

I'm not dead, Fran. I won't leave you, not now, not ever. We belong to each other.

I sobbed over him as his chest rose, his lungs wheezing as he dragged air into them. *There you go again, getting all pushy with me. I haven't said I want you, let alone belong to you.* I wiped my eyes on my sleeve as I bent over his face. His lips twitched.

Ah, Fran, what would I do without you?

Probably date a bunch of really pretty girls with no brains who oohed and aahed over your gorgeous self and very cool motorcycle, and didn't appreciate you at all for your ability to have a hole punched through your chest and still be able to make all sorts of he-man-type comments.

Probably. I guess it's good I have you.

"I guess it is," I said, and pressed a little kiss to his lips.

Chapter Thirteen

"This is all your fault."

Whump!

"It most certainly isn't!"

Thud!

"Yes, it is. You're his older sister; if you hadn't let him brainwash you into thinking that you couldn't do things by yourself"—*Whack! Screech*—"he wouldn't be so Mr. 'I'm the Dark One; I will fix everything' with everyone, and we wouldn't be here now, having to beat up a demon."

Slam!

"That is totally unjustified!" Imogen lowered one end of the board she was using to beat the demon on the head, and glared at me. "I never said I couldn't do things myself; it's just easier to have Benedikt take care of them for me. He knows perfectly well that I could have taken care of Elvis if I wanted to."

The demon started to snarl out a curse that would damn us both to hell as it lunged for Imogen, its hands dripping from where it had attacked Ben. I walloped it on the back with the tire iron I'd pulled from Imogen's trunk. "Oh, yeah, right. I am *so* not believing that."

The demon spun around and jumped at me, a wicked knife suddenly appearing in its hand. I gave myself a quick mental lecture about not paying attention and jumped out of the way just as it swung the knife toward me. Imogen did a fabulous martial arts kick that sent the knife spinning helplessly away. The demon screeched again. "I could have! I just thought it was more expedient to have Benedikt do it. He enjoys doing those sorts of things."

"Expedient?" The demon jerked the tire iron out of my hands, throwing me into the car parked nearby. I shook the stars from my eyes as it hurled itself at Imogen. Without waiting for common sense to kick in, I threw myself on its back, and slapped my hands over its eyes. It hurled oaths at me, invoking the name of its demon lord as Imogen avoided the spikey end of the tire iron. She walloped it across the knees with a board, yelling at me to get out of the way. The demon crumpled up into a little ball. "How expedient is it for your brother to be lying in the field over there with more than half of his blood drained out of his body?"

"Correction," a tired voice said behind me. Ben limped into the circle of light cast by the street lamp, one hand over his chest. The wound no longer dripped blood, but he looked awful. "I'm no longer lying in the field. I'm here to get rid of the demon. Stand aside, both of you."

I made a moue at Imogen. She raised her eyebrows at me. "Oh, very well, I will take a modest amount of the blame for his being the way he is, but not"—she swung at the demon with her hunk of wood, connecting with its shoulders. It screamed and tried to cut her with a broken piece of glass it picked up from the side of the road. I kicked the glass from its hands, my whole body hurting from the battle. The demon finally must have had enough, though, because it just laid there on the ground, a quivering, stinking mass of evil intentions and demonic power—"not for everything. Dark Ones are naturally arrogant. You're just going to have to deal with that particular trait as best you can."

"Imogen! Fran!" Ben snarled, or tried to snarl. It came out kind of a really mean whimper. "You must leave, both of you. I will deal with this situation."

I stopped glaring down at demon long enough to push Ben up against the hood of Imogen's car. "Sit down before you pass out."

"I will not allow you—"

"Will you just let us take care of this, please?" I waved toward where Imogen was jumping up and down to avoid one last attack by the demon. "If you'll notice, we're doing a pretty good job of taking care of ourselves—and you."

"Fran does have a point, little brother. We are quite capable of taking care of this evil one, although I do appreciate your desire to protect us." She whomped the demon upside the head with the board. It fell over, moaning and twitching a couple of times before it finally gave up trying to kill us.

"Fran doesn't know what she's talking about," Ben said, pushing himself away from the car. "She's never even seen a demon before, let alone know how to fight one."

"I know now," I said, setting down the tire iron I had reclaimed to tick off the items on my fingers. "I know that demons don't like steel. It burns them."

"Steel?" Imogen drew a ward over the demon that made it arch up backward, scream twice, then disappear into a plume of really nasty-smelling black smoke. She dusted off her hands and walked toward us. "Not steel, silver."

"But Elvis told me . . . Oh. He lied."

She brushed her hair back over her shoulder and smiled at us both. She didn't look at all like someone who had just beaten a demon to a pulp. "I suspect he's lied about a great many things."

"Hmm. I guess that means he's the thief, too." Something nudged my mind, a thought that wanted attention, but I had something more important to do.

"Go on, Fran. I think Benedikt needs to hear just how much you've learned."

"Oh." I smiled back at her. "Well, let's see . . . there's also the fact that when a demon takes a human form, it's bound by the strengths and weaknesses of that form, so if you can run it down with a car and break its legs—"

"And drive a dagger of pure silver through its heart—I'm afraid that did more damage than the car, Fran."

"—and drive a dagger of pure silver through its heart, you will disable the demon enough to allow you to beat it up."

"Even then you have to weaken the body significantly so the demon is forced to leave it and return to the fiery pit from which it came."

"Right." I nodded and turned to face Ben. "So see?

We didn't need you. We defeated the demon all on our own. *We* saved *you.*"

"That's not how it's supposed to work," he said, frowning at me.

"It's 2005, not 1705," I said, patting him on the shoulder. "Learn to deal with it."

We didn't get back to the Faire for another half hour. Ben had to replace some of the blood he'd lost. I worried that he was going to need me to play blood donor—and I wasn't sure how I was going to explain to him that although I didn't want him to die, I wasn't sure I wanted to be bound to him for all eternity, either—but luckily Imogen offered him her wrist. It was the first time I'd seen Ben . . . *drinking.* His teeth flashed as he bit her wrist, giving me a brief, momentary glimpse of two long canine teeth before his mouth closed over her flesh.

"Wow," I said, watching him, feeling like an intruder on something private, and yet unable to look away. "That's pretty wild. Does it . . . uh . . . hurt?"

"No," Imogen said, stroking Ben's hair with her free hand. She kissed the top of his head. "It brings me pleasure to give him life. Just as it will you someday."

Uh . . . not going to go there.

While Ben sucked down some much-needed blood, I went out to round up Tesla, who was happily grazing now that the demon was gone. "You were pretty impressive there for an old guy," I said, patting him on the neck. He walked along quietly, nuzzling me now and again as if he hoped an apple might magically appear. "You can have two when we get back home," I promised.

We had a brief skirmish when Ben, looking a bit

better, insisted that I ride back with Imogen in her car while he led Tesla, but in the end I settled the matter by scrambling onto Tesla's back and nudging him off toward the Faire while Ben was still tossing out orders.

He caught up with me a few feet later. Imogen's car zipped by us, giving me enough light to see the furious scowl on Ben's face. "Maybe you should ride and I should walk. You're the one who's been injured."

His hand clamped down on my leg. "Stay where you are. I can walk."

He was moving a bit easier now, no longer hunched over like his chest was hurting him. I remembered how quickly he'd healed his blisters, but even so, the size of the hole that had been punched through him was awfully big. I let Tesla amble along at a slow pace, glancing down at the man who walked silently beside me.

"Do I get to see your fangs?"

"No."

He didn't even look at me when he said it. What a poop. "How come?"

"You don't have a need to see them."

"I saved your life; that should count for something. I want to see your fangs."

"I did not need you to save me. I would have recovered on my own. I would have defeated the demon."

I snorted. "That's not what Imogen says."

He walked along, scowling, but silent.

"I bet Imogen's seen your fangs."

Tesla dropped his head to graze. I slipped off his back and touched Ben's arm. "I bet all your other girlfriends have seen your fangs."

"They have not." Ben turned to me, his black brows

drawn together. His hair was loose, a dark curtain of silk around his face, his eyes a beautiful oak with tiny sparkly gold bits. "I do not make it a habit to show . . . *other* girlfriends?"

I smiled and slid my hands over his shoulders, into the cool length of his hair. "I thought maybe since I saved your life and all, we might try this boyfriend/girlfriend thing for a bit. Just to see how it feels."

His arms went around my back, pulling me toward him. I leaned against him very, very gently, not wanting to harm his healing wound. "You're going to drive me mad, aren't you? You're going to torment me for years while you try to decide whether or not you wish to fulfill your destiny with me."

"Maybe," I said, smiling against his lips. "Are you going to show me your fangs?"

"No," he said, his breath warm against my mouth. "I'll let you feel them."

His lips moved over mine, encouraging me to investigate. I did, hesitantly, unsure whether or not I really wanted what he offered, but in the end I allowed him to tease me into tasting him. The tip of my tongue slid over his front teeth, curling under to feel the points of two long, very sharp canine teeth.

Elvis disappeared. When Ben and I walked Tesla back to the Faire, it was business as usual . . . with the exception of Mom and her gang running around trying to force amulets on everyone. We dragged Absinthe and Peter (and Soren) from the band tent, collecting everyone in Mom's tent to give an update on what happened.

"I think Elvis is your thief," I told Absinthe and Peter. "I'm not sure, but I think he did it as a way to get Imogen."

Imogen frowned. "Why on earth would he think driving the Faire into the ground would win my favor?"

"Well . . ." I chewed on my lip and glanced at Ben. He sat in the shadows, a large, black shape that oddly enough exuded comfort and support. He had faith in me, even when I didn't. That gave my mental processes a little boost. "I think his plan was to push the Faire into a desperate situation, then offer to buy it himself with the money he'd stolen."

Imogen snorted.

"I know, it doesn't make a lot of sense to me, either, but he was desperate to have you. I think he felt in some weird way that if he owned the Faire, he'd own you, too."

"But how did he take the money, eh? How did he get into the safe vithout my knowing it?" Absinthe asked.

I took a deep breath. Mom and the other witches were sitting on the ground, clutching their amulets. Mom gave me an encouraging smile. It was kind of weird being the focus of so many people's attention, but at the same time, it felt good. Kind of like they accepted me, as though they valued what I had to say. It wasn't the same as when I tried to blend in at school, but it was . . . all right. Good, even.

"He didn't get into your safe," I said, the final pieces of the puzzle sliding into place. The thing that had been bothering me all day finally came into focus.

I turned to Peter. "You must have known that Elvis knew magic, right?"

"He knew sleight of hand." Peter shrugged. "Close magic, yes. Card tricks."

"Substituting one thing for another as part of a trick, right? That's what he did today at the hospital."

"Yes, that is what sleight of hand is."

I turned to Absinthe. "How would you put the money away for the night? That is, what would you do before you put it into the safe?"

Absinthe's eyes narrowed. She still looked at me suspiciously, but ever since I'd come walking back into the Faire with Ben's arm around me, she'd given me a wide berth. "I took the money from Peter and counted it, tallying it against the slips from each employee."

"Where would you count it?"

"In my trailer."

I glanced at Ben. He smiled.

"While you did that, were you alone?"

Her frown grew blacker. "No, sometimes Karl would help, sometimes . . ."

"Elvis?" I asked when she stopped.

She said something that even in German I understood. "That pig! I will roast his guts! I will cut out his heart and eat it! He stole from me!"

"Sleight of hand," I said to Soren, who looked puzzled. "Elvis was a master at taking an item and switching it with another one. I bet he had some of those money pouches all made up with newspaper, so all he had to do was switch them when Absinthe was looking the other way. Then she'd tuck them away in the safe, never knowing that she'd been robbed."

It was Peter's turn to swear. Everyone left a few minutes after that, Absinthe promising dark vengeance on Elvis's guts, Peter muttering about calling the police, Mom and her gang to hold another emergency circle to see if they couldn't bring down Elvis, or at least blight him with boils or a really nasty rash.

Soren gave me a pitiful look just before he followed his dad out of the tent. "You were supposed to let me help you find out who was the thief. I'm your sidekick."

"Sorry, it just kind of happened. Next time you can be the detective and I'll be the sidekick."

He glanced at Ben, then shrugged and limped off after Peter.

"Tomorrow we shall be on our way to Budapest, where I will be able to shop until I drop." Imogen slid off the table she was sitting on, stretched, and blew a kiss to Ben. "I will need a new silver dagger. I shall buy you one as well, Fran. Thank you for what you did. I believe I will go and see if Jan is still here. He has many qualities I have not yet investigated. . . ."

She drifted off. I looked at Ben, gnawing on my lip. I'd kissed a vampire, survived Absinthe's attempt to get into my mind, and had helped beat up a demon—surely I could do this, too. "So, um . . . are you . . . uh . . . you know, going to be hanging around with us in Budapest, or do you have to do stuff somewhere else?"

He stood up and cupped my jaw in his hands, pressing his lips to my forehead. Mom gasped in the background. "I must go hunt down Elvis, but once I have found him, I will return."

He stared into my eyes for a second, then left. Just walked out of there and left. I stood there with my jaw hanging around my knees for a moment, then realized what he'd done.

That rat!

I ran out of the tent, grabbing the back of his shirt as he strode down the center aisle. He ignored my tugging and marched onward. "Hey! Didn't we just have a talk about you being all macho and feeling like you have to save Imogen and me all the time? No one says you need to hunt down Elvis; Peter is going to call the police—"

"I am a Dark One. He is a threat to Imogen, and now that you have identified him as the thief, he is a threat to you. I cannot tolerate that threat."

"Do you know what you are? You're just a great, big chauvinist pig; that's what you are. My mother's told me about guys like you."

"You will not argue with me about this—"

"I will so argue about this, and don't you tell me what to do. I'm in charge of my life, not you—"

"You will stay with your mother and Imogen, and you will not endanger yourself again—"

"I never was in danger, you pigheaded boob! I had the ward to protect me. You were the one lying on the field with his guts spread out all over—"

"I am a Dark One. You are my Beloved. It is my right to protect you—"

" 'I am a Dark One; I am a Dark One. . . . ' Of all the hooey! You are so full of it. You know what? My *next* boyfriend is going to think I can do anything. He's going to worship the ground I walk on."

"I worship you—"

GOT FANGS?

"Ha!"

"I do!"

"Double ha with frogs on it!"

You know, I have to admit, I'm kind of looking forward to the rest of the summer. I may still be Fran the Freak Queen, and I may still not fit in anywhere but with a bunch of fellow freaks, but somehow that doesn't seem quite as bad as it used to be.

Who knows, I may just survive this year after all. Stranger things have happened.

EYELINER OF THE GODS
KATIE MAXWELL

To Whom It May Concern:

If you find this letter, it means that I, January James, have fallen down the burial shaft of the Tomb of Tekhen and Tekhnet where I'm spending a month working as a conservator, and am probably lying at the bottom, dead from a broken leg and thirst. . . .

To whoever finds my sand-scoured, withered corpse:

I'm dead. It's the mummy's curse. Don't blame Seth, he was just trying to help, even if everyone does say he's the reincarnation of an evil Egyptian god. He's not. I know, because no one who kisses like he does can be truly evil.

Help! I'm stuck in Egypt with a pushy girl named Chloe, a cursed bracelet, and a hottie who makes my toes curl. . . .

Dorchester Publishing Co., Inc.
P.O. Box 6640
Wayne, PA 19087-8640

5378-0
$5.99 US/$7.99 CAN

Please add $2.50 for shipping and handling for the first book and $.75 for each additional book. NY and PA residents, add appropriate sales tax. No cash, stamps, or CODs. Canadian orders require an extra $2.00 for shipping and handling and must be paid in U.S. dollars. Prices and availability subject to change. **Payment must accompany all orders.**

Name: _____

Address: _____

City: _____ State: _____ Zip: _____

E-mail: _____

I have enclosed $_____ in payment for the checked book(s).

CHECK OUT OUR WEBSITE! www.smoochya.com
_____ Please send me a free catalog.

The Year My Life Went Down the Loo
by Katie Maxwell

Subject: The Grotty and the Fabu (No, it's not a song.)
From: Mrs.Oded@btelecom.co.uk
To: Dru@seattlegrrl.com

Things That Really Irk My Pickle About Living in England

- The school uniform
- Piddlington-on-the-weld (I will forever be known as Emily from *Piddlesville)*
- Marmite (It's yeast sludge! GACK!)
- The ghost in my underwear drawer (Spectral hands fondling my bras—enough said!)
- No malls! What are these people *thinking???*

Things That Keep Me From Flying Home to Seattle for Good Coffee

- Aidan (*Hunkalicious!*)
- Devon (*Droolworthy?* Understatement of the year!*)
- Fang (He puts the *num* in *nummy!*)
- Holly (Any girl who hunts movie stars with me—and Oded Fehr *will be mine*—is a friend for life.)
- Über-coolio Polo Club (Where the snogging is FINE!)

Dorchester Publishing Co., Inc.
P.O. Box 6640   5251-2
Wayne, PA 19087-8640 $5.99 US/$7.99 CAN

Please add $2.50 for shipping and handling for the first book and $.75 for each additional book.
NY and PA residents, add appropriate sales tax. No cash, stamps, or CODs. Canadian orders
require $2.00 for shipping and handling and must be paid in U.S. dollars. Prices and availability
subject to change. **Payment must accompany all orders.**

Name: _____
Address: _____
City: _____ State: _____ Zip: _____
E-mail: _____

CHECK OUT OUR WEBSITE! www.smoochya.com
_____ *Please send me a free catalog.*

They Wear WHAT Under Their Kilts?

by Katie Maxwell

Subject: Emily's Glossary for People Who Haven't Been to Scotland
From: Mrs.Legolas@kiltnet.com
To: Dru@seattlegrrl.com

Faffing about: running around doing nothing. In other words, spending a month supposedly doing work experience on a Scottish sheep farm, but really spending days on Kilt Watch at the nearest castle.

Schottie: Scottish Hottie, also known as Ruaraidh.

Mad schnoogles: the British way of saying big smoochy kisses. Will admit it sounds v. smart to say it that way.

Bunch of yobbos: a group of mindless idiots. In Scotland, can also mean sheep.

Stooshie: uproar, as in, "If Holly thinks she can take Ruaraidh from me without causing a stooshie, she's out of her mind!"

Sheep dip: not an appetizer.

Dorchester Publishing Co., Inc.
P.O. Box 6640   5258-X
Wayne, PA 19087-8640 $5.99 US/$7.99 CAN

Please add $2.50 for shipping and handling for the first book and $.75 for each additional book. NY and PA residents, add appropriate sales tax. No cash, stamps, or CODs. Canadian orders require $2.00 for shipping and handling and must be paid in U.S. dollars. Prices and availability subject to change. Payment must accompany all orders.

Name: _____
Address: _____
City: _____ State: _____ Zip: _____
E-mail: _____

CHECK OUT OUR WEBSITE! www.smoochya.com
_____ Please send me a free catalog.

What's French For "EW!"?

KATIE MAXWELL

Subject: Emily's Handy Phrases For Spring Break in Paris
From: Em-the-enforcer@englandrocks.com
To: Dru@seattlegrrl.com

*J'apprendrais par coeur plutôt le Klingon qu'essaye d'apprendre
le français en deux semaines.*
I would rather memorize Klingon than try to
learn French in two weeks.

Vous voulez que je mange un escargot?
You want me to *EAT* a snail?!?

*Vous êtes nummy, mais mon petit ami est le roi des hotties,
et il vient à Paris seulement pour me voir!*
You are nummy, but my boyfriend is the king of hotties,
and he's coming to Paris just to see me!

Dorchester Publishing Co., Inc.
P.O. Box 6640   5297-0
Wayne, PA 19087-8640 $5.99 US/$7.99 CAN

Please add $2.50 for shipping and handling for the first book and $.75 for each additional book.
NY and PA residents, add appropriate sales tax. No cash, stamps, or CODs. Canadian orders
require an extra $2.00 for shipping and handling and must be paid in U.S. dollars. Prices and
availability subject to change. **Payment must accompany all orders.**

Name: _____
Address: _____
City: _____ State: _____ Zip: _____
E-mail: _____

CHECK OUT OUR WEBSITE! www.smoochya.com
_____ Please send me a free catalog.

SUPER ★ WHAT? ★

JAX ABBOTT

THE TOP FIVE WAYS NOT TO START YOUR FIRST DAY AT A NEW HIGH SCHOOL:

1. Tell the hottest guy in class that he reminds you of an elf.

2. Get *enormongo* cramps.

3. Annoy one of the Populars.

4. Make even the geeks pity you.

5. Finally get the superpowers you thought you'd *never* have and explode all the windows in English class.

Jessie was SO not wearing tights and a cape!

- -

Dorchester Publishing Co., Inc.
P.O. Box 6640
Wayne, PA 19087-8640

_____5385-3
$5.99 US/$7.99 CAN

Please add $2.50 for shipping and handling for the first book and $.75 for each additional book. NY and PA residents, add appropriate sales tax. No cash, stamps, or CODs. Canadian orders require an extra $2.00 for shipping and handling and must be paid in U.S. dollars. Prices and availability subject to change. **Payment must accompany all orders.**

Name: _____

Address: _____

City: _____ State: _____ Zip: _____

E-mail: _____

I have enclosed $_____ in payment for the checked book(s).

CHECK OUT OUR WEBSITE! www.smoochya.com
_____ Please send me a free catalog.

THE REAL DEAL

Unscripted

Amy Kaye

Thanks to the reality-TV show that records her junior year in excruciating detail, Claire Marangello gets her big break: her own version of the TV show and a starring role in a Broadway musical. Plus Jeb, a way-hot co-star who seems to like her *that* way, and a half sister she didn't know she had. It's everything she's ever dreamed of.

Or is it a total nightmare? Her sister seems to be drifting away. Claire's not sure she can trust Jeb and his weird celebrity-centered world. The director seems to hate her; the dance steps are harder than she'd ever imagined. Claire's about to learn that while being a Broadway star is a challenge, real life has twists and turns harder than any onstage choreography and is totally . . . *UNSCRIPTED*.

Dorchester Publishing Co., Inc.
P.O. Box 6640
Wayne, PA 19087-8640

__5315-2
$5.99 US/$7.99 CAN

Please add $2.50 for shipping and handling for the first book and $.75 for each additional book. NY and PA residents, add appropriate sales tax. No cash, stamps, or CODs. Canadian orders require an extra $2.00 for shipping and handling and must be paid in U.S. dollars. Prices and availability subject to change. **Payment must accompany all orders.**

Name: _____

Address: _____

City: _____ State: _____ Zip: _____

E-mail: _____

I have enclosed $_____ in payment for the checked book(s).

CHECK OUT OUR WEBSITE! www.smoochya.com
____ *Please send me a free catalog.*

Didn't want this book to end?

There's more waiting at **www.smoochya.com**:

Win FREE books and makeup!
Read excerpts from other books!
Chat with the authors!
Horoscopes!
Quizzes!

 Bringing you the books on everyone's lips!